KIMANI
ROMANCE
TM

SO-BBB-054

ISBN-13:978-0-373-86287-0

5²⁴⁹⁵

EAN

KIMANI ROMANCE

RACING HEARTS

MICHELLE MONKOU

He tapped his glass
with Erin's again and she smiled.

Somehow she managed to sip the champagne with the sexiest smile he'd ever seen. The liquid wet her lips, offering her mouth with a moistened pucker.

He leaned over and responded. He kissed her with a madcap intention to simply match her pucker with his puckered lips. Fun and games, that's all.

More science and physics came into effect. The innocent kiss exploded the nerve endings in his mouth. There had to be some law about attraction. Instead of losing sensation, as expected from an explosion of the senses, his mouth acted as a superconductor, sending and receiving sensually erotic messages.

Craving more, he tested the waters again. This time he discarded the pucker for a lock-and-load kiss sealing her mouth with a tender determination. Every time she responded to his attention, he pulled her tighter toward him.

Her parted lips invited him to enter at his own risk. Something basic, more than adrenaline, but more primal and uncivilized, zipped through his blood. Its energy pumped through his system like a fast-moving drug that saturated his heart, soul and body.

Books by Michelle Monkou

Harlequin Kimani Romance

Sweet Surrender
Here and Now
Straight to the Heart
No One But You
Gamble on Love
Only in Paradise
Trail of Kisses
The Millionaire's Ultimate Catch
If I Had You
Racing Hearts

MICHELLE MONKOU

became a world traveler at the age of three when she left her birthplace of London, England, and moved to Guyana, South America. She then moved to the United States as a young teen.

Michelle was nominated for the 2003 Emma Award for Favorite New Author, and continues to write romances with complex characters and intricate plots. For further information visit her website at www.michellemonkou.com or contact her at michellemonkou@comcast.net.

RACING
HEARTS

MICHELLE MONKOU

HARLEQUIN®

entertain, enrich, inspire™

Thank you to the teachers and nuns
at Stella Maris Primary School in Georgetown, Guyana,
for nurturing my creative spirit.

Recycling programs
for this product may
not exist in your area.

ISBN-13: 978-0-373-86287-0

RACING HEARTS

Dear Reader,

Racing Hearts is a hot romance: sexy, seductive race-car driver and a no-nonsense, feisty doctor; adrenaline-pumping speeds and dangerous curves, on the track and in the bed; and high-stakes drama to push love to its limit.

I've loved writing my millionaire heroes. These gorgeous men are used to having their way. When arrogance is added to the mix, the heroes walk on stage with swag and sexiness, ready for any seductive mission.

However, their dreams may be lost in an instant, delayed, or threatened by saboteurs. How do you manage obstacles? Do you take a step back to ponder? Do you figure a way around, looking at pros and cons? Do you take a deep breath and plunge ahead, dealing with consequences later?

Whatever your style, don't forget to dream; don't be afraid to achieve. In 2013 you can make it happen!

Blessings,

Michelle
http://facebook.com/michellemonkou

Chapter 1

Marc Newton wished he could run his race car business without sponsors. An illogical thought considering how much cross-marketing was done, making each side dependent on the other. Besides, the cold, hard reality for him came down to his ability to generate revenue. Especially now that his body threatened to punk out on his plan to dominate the auto racing landscape.

The business relationship, however, exacted a heavy debt. Sponsors wanted a chunk of his flesh with their legal teams pushing meetings that elicited endorsements for their various products, crafting deals for bigger profit margins and pushing their cause for partnerships in other business ventures.

One day he awoke and his name was more than his identity. His fairly new iconic status had escalated on a steep incline and was now a viable brand. Sports pundits predicted that his income potential had only hit the tip of the iceberg. Being one of the top fifteen drivers in the National Car Racing Federation guaranteed him financial success.

In the competitive inner sanctum of the industry, a few critical sportscasters shared their belief that he hadn't earned his stripes yet. That was real B.S. He'd earned every accolade by rolling up his sleeves and working hard, putting in the long hours running his business and being disciplined. No way would he apologize for his success.

His rise to the esteemed top fifteen started as a driver struggling to get experience first in the local and regional races and then on the bigger tracks and speedways. He wasn't part of a family dynasty, nor had he nurtured business contacts to give him a leg up on the inner workings. Rather it was through dogged determination that he'd earned enough money to take the next step and serve as president of his own small company, Newton Enterprises. He also took on the double role as the key driver for his fleet.

His dream hadn't changed since the first time he spent the day with his father at a car race. Nothing beat the roar of the engines, the electrifying speed of the cars shooting out onto the track. Each time he got behind the wheel, he channeled that rush of adrenaline to fuel his senses as he strategized his path to the finish line.

Some days he got to the finish line with a few bumps. Then there were those days when nothing fell into place and his car hurtled like a bumper car down the track. The last race shook and rattled his body like a rag doll between a rottweiler's teeth. A reaggravated neck injury now had his board of directors and sponsors wringing their hands like nervous Nellies. The investors pushed him to get a quick checkup by one of their recommended specialty doctors.

For Marc, the whole ordeal was a big waste of his time. He was willing to try anything to get out of the doctor's appointment. However, since he couldn't, the next strategy was to twist the female doctor around his finger. A flash of his smile and wave of tickets usually netted the results he wanted. And now he wanted a quick exam and an official release to race.

"Mr. Newton, the doctor will see you now."

Marc followed the nurse through the door that led him deeper into the doctor's lair. The walls of the medical suite were painted the warm, creamy yellow of honeydew melon and decorated with framed abstract art, but they did little to calm him. Unlike the nerves that fairly popped as he prepared for a race, the nervous spikes of dread slinking down his legs had nothing to do with precompetition jitters or the need for speed.

Doctors, hospitals, threats of dire prognoses always seem to touch on his childhood fears. He didn't want to go down that dark road. The Do Not Enter sign spoke only to him. Over time, he'd learned to heed the directive.

The nurse escorted him into the examination room, chatting about the hot North Carolina summer they'd just endured. Folks around the city didn't usually grumble about fall's entrance in September. However, Marc knew at the end of the racing season, the weather would take a sharp turn to an unpredictable, icy wintry mix.

He submitted to the thermometer, weight scale and blood pressure cuff. Not that he had much of a choice once he'd decided to come into the office.

The nurse ran through the preliminary checklist of his vitals. By now her conversation had turned to her thoughts regarding car racing. Her opinion that it was a dangerous sport received validation, she claimed, upon noticing a few of his old wounds.

Where the heck was the doctor? He wanted out—fast.

On cue, a light knock on the examination door preempted the nurse's lecture. "Mr. Newton, it's Dr. Wilson."

"Come in." Marc focused on the door. Now he was curious to see the owner of the husky voice colored with a sexy lilt.

He didn't have long to wait. She entered, armed with a wide smile and an extended hand. She shook his with a confident grasp and instantly he recognized someone used to being in control. Her gaze assessed him, as if collecting data to ponder for an eventual decision. Despite the smiling greeting, she wore her cool professionalism like an additional layer of clothing.

Marc mentally pulled up short. The warm, gooey voice hung in the air like false advertising. The doctor's no-nonsense demeanor didn't partner well with her warm, sultry voice. Charming her might prove difficult. She'd already turned her attention to the computer with his medical file.

"Doc, look, I know that I have to come to you because sponsors have that in my contract. But I'm fine. Look at my vitals. I'm a vision of good health." He grinned. "Good looks, too." He raised his chin slightly. No woman could resist him. Some turned his way fast and held on tight. Some turned his way slowly, taking a little more effort on his part. But sooner or later he had them all eating out of his hand. He had that knack. The promise of a challenge stirred his competitive spirit.

Why should this doctor be an exception, even if she wasn't really his type?

"I have your images from the latest MRI," Dr. Wilson said.

"And…?" He didn't like the fact that she hadn't responded to his light flirtation. Nor did he like her serious countenance as she pulled up his file and leaned toward the computer monitor. She pointed at data on the screen, tracing the line of information. Her forehead wore a deep furrow.

When she was done reading, she stepped back from the monitor and then turned to him. "Your neck is heavily bruised." Her fingers trailed a path along the back of his neck from the base into the hairline.

"That's all?" He twitched his shoulders away from her touch.

"It wouldn't be such a big deal if it hadn't been accompanied by your second concussion. What your body needs to get over this hurdle is rest. You need to heal."

"Uh-huh." Marc felt his phone vibrate in his pocket. His busy life was knocking, waiting for his attention. But the steely-eyed gaze his doctor cast on him warned him that multitasking wouldn't be appreciated. His hand remained in his pocket, covering the phone.

The doctor pulled out a form and began writing. "Do you have any questions?"

"You said that I needed to heal." He glanced at the form. "I don't think I need written instructions for that."

"This is going to you and the insurance company with my recommendation that you sit out racing for two weeks. Then we can recheck and get you back in the saddle. I will also recommend that you have a limited number of physical therapy sessions."

"No way." Marc shot up from the examining table. He didn't care that he'd momentarily startled her. She was about to sideline him with the stroke of that pen. Didn't she realize what she was going to do to his career?

"Mr. Newton, relax."

"Look, stop calling me that. You're about to wreck my life. Drop the formality, please. I'm Marc."

"Fine." The doctor's mouth tightened into a disapproving line. Her eyebrows arched over sharp, dark brown eyes. "Marc, I'm aware that you make a living from your driving. My goal is to make sure that you are able to continue driving safely and in good health. Right now, you're nursing some pretty serious injuries."

"I feel fine."

"The images don't lie. I interpret them, give you my expert opinion and provide my recommendations."

He'd pushed and she'd pushed right back.

Marc tried a different approach. "If the physical therapy works in a week, then I can get behind the wheel and perform my practice runs that following week." He stated his opinion, rather than asking for hers.

"I can't say how quickly you will heal. Nor am I going to rush your recovery."

"But if I'm clear, then you can't block me?" Marc wanted to be perfectly clear of the rules.

"I wish you wouldn't take the attitude that I'm restraining you. It's not my purpose or my goal."

Marc shrugged. He didn't want to argue semantics. Only his release mattered.

"So, if you don't have any further questions, I'll have the nurse schedule your therapy sessions."

"Who's conducting the therapy?" He didn't care if he sounded grumpy. Her matter-of-fact tone stirred his desire to argue with her.

"It will be me."

"Really?" What the heck? Couldn't he get a break? "Isn't it below your pay grade to play with my neck?" He remembered how he'd barely been able to stand her touch a few moments ago. Not that the sensation had been unpleasant. Quite the opposite. Darn it, this was his doctor.

"This is my practice. I'm perfectly able to work at any level. Allows me to stay on top of my clients' progress. In your case, my close attention is mandatory." She clicked her pen rapidly. "Do you have any objections?" Her eyes blazed at him, as if willing him to say something to offend her further.

Marc had lots of objections, but he wasn't about to lay them at Dr. Wilson's feet. Petite as she might be, her iron will seemed to have a tall reach. Plan B hadn't been ironed out yet.

"Good. Here's your paperwork. It was nice meeting you. My contact information is listed on the paperwork. Please call me if you experience any pain. Otherwise, I will see you again for therapy." She offered her hand once again. He reluctantly shook it.

"Thanks." Marc folded the paper and clenched it in his fist. He couldn't wait to get out of her office.

Other meetings were on his schedule for the day. Top priority was to get on the phone to his manager of operations to set up a meeting with the most influential member of his board of directors. However, taking care of the pressing issue of the doctor's power over his ability to drive prevented him from thinking about anything else.

Checking his phone, he saw that his manager had already taken care of things. Lionel's text informed him that a quick meeting with the board member was already scheduled. Marc had fifteen minutes to get to the office. That was all the time he needed to get across Raleigh to Edgar Pace's office. By the time he arrived, his foul mood had enough time to percolate to an angry boil. His mood could easily be compared to a dark summer storm of crackling anger and thunderous frustration.

He walked into the glass-and-chrome office building that headquartered Edgar's aeronautical engineering business. Investing in Newton Enterprises was a side venture, an outlet for Edgar's enthusiasm for car racing. Their paths had crossed at a charity golf game several years ago. An easy business partnership followed.

"Here to see Edgar." Marc had to pass three security checkpoints before he finally stood at Edgar's secretary's work area. She nodded, had him sign in again and then indicated that he should follow her to Edgar's palatial office.

"Marc, come on in." While Marc settled himself, Edgar continued, "You look like you could kick someone's behind just for saying howdy do."

"Pretty much. I suppose Lionel gave you a headsup?" Edgar nodded. "What the heck is up with the new doctor?" Marc barged on with his irritation. "She wants to sideline me for therapy. I'm supposed to be racing in two weeks. But she doesn't seem to give a rat's—"

"The checkup was only a formality."

"Not in her opinion. The woman would put Mary Poppins to shame—all wrapped up in rules and regulations with a crusader's spirit." He didn't mention the delicate features, graceful arm movements or the way she walked, as if she trained in ballet. And he certainly wouldn't mention the sexy, husky voice that could deliver bad news with a velvety touch. Not fair. Not normal. Not his type.

Edgar waved away his objections. "She comes highly recommended."

"I'm not questioning her credentials or reputation. I have a problem with someone taking full control over what I can and can't do. It's my damn body."

"Sponsors may beg to differ on that point." Dressed in a custom-made suit, Edgar looked the role of savvy deal maker and sharklike deal breaker. He flashed a toothy grin while twisting a thick diamond ring on his pinky finger. "Relax. We'll get around this. It wouldn't hurt for you to do the rehab anyway."

Marc stewed over the nudge to play nice. He hadn't won a race since early in the season or placed high in the last four races. His car had been clipped, pushed or smashed against the wall with increasing frequency. The rigors of the last skirmish had had longer effects on his body. He'd had to keep ice packs on his shoulders and heat on his back. Now concussions had to be added to the list of injuries. Still, he wasn't happy about relinquishing his future, even for a little bit, to a pushy doctor with a nervous habit with her pen.

Erin Wilson shook her head when Marc marched out of the examining room. It was either shake her head or shake her fist at the arrogant piece of work that had occupied her last hour. His departure seemed to sap the electric charge in the room. The weight of his mighty ego actually caused a physical reaction that magnified in small spaces.

Not many people flustered her. When she met with a

patient, she came ready to use her knowledge, whether medical or life experience, to form a partnership toward their better health. In some cases, patients with an active lifestyle were in denial when faced with their new, modified abilities. Their disbelief then took a sharp turn to frustration. Emotions tended to run high and at extremes. She became the enemy. Such daunting challenges motivated her with a stronger determination to help her patients adjust and move forward.

Marc Newton, however, made that challenge feel less like a speed bump and more of a boulder-size problem. She clicked her pen furiously. He may be the king of the speedway, but she was queen of her medical office. So, he could put away the sexy grin, penetrating glare and off-the-chain sex appeal.

One thing she wanted to prove to his oversize male charisma was that she wasn't buying into it. She wasn't going to swoon like an empty-headed bimbo who served no other purpose than being someone's sex kitten. She adjusted her doctor coat and clicked her pen several times before putting it in her pocket and heading to her next patient.

Nothing about her screamed an easy lay. She made sure that her image stayed at a professional level. Otherwise, respect would be hard to earn. There were always some patients who tried to cross the line, though.

Patients like the silver-tongued race car driver with the killer smile.

Erin tended her patient, then continued working through the day. Her thoughts drifted to Marc Newton a few more times than she deemed appropriate. It wasn't the first time that she'd had a physically attractive male patient, she told herself. With Marc, however, she couldn't quite put her finger on the elusive quality that she found sexy and that had the power to turn her on.

"Hey, sis, rough day? What's got you so deep in thought that you didn't hear me calling your name?"

Erin looked up to see Lani, her younger sister, standing in the office doorway, twirling her car keys on one finger. "Hey, yourself. What are you doing here? Did I forget about a meeting with you?"

Lani shook her head. "I was in the area and wanted to stop in."

"Oh, no." Erin shook her head. She pointedly moved her pocketbook off her desk and placed it in the drawer.

"Stop being a meanie. I've got money," Lani whined.

"For the moment."

"Whatever. I have boyfriend issues." Lani scrunched her face.

"I'm so not the person to help you." Erin rolled her eyes at her sister's problem.

Though she and Lani were opposites in build and personality, emotionally they were as close as if they were twins, and they had the uncanny ability to communicate nonverbally. Although Lani was two years younger, she was taller with a thicker frame. Unlike Erin, she had an extremely outgoing personality. Lani's verve for the lighter side of life and her off-color sense of humor had magnetic powers that drew many suitors.

"Why can't you help me? You give good advice. You think about stuff and think and rethink. Plus you don't get all emotional. My girlfriends get crazy and wound up. Next thing you know, they'd want to go kick my boyfriend's butt."

"Based on the kinds of craziness you get into, a butt kicking might not be a bad idea." Erin wondered when her sister would mature and calm down.

"Oh, stop." Lani slid into the chair in front of Erin's desk and planted her feet on its edge. One have-you-lost-your-darn-mind glare from Erin and she promptly lowered her feet to the floor. "You don't have any appointments this afternoon. I checked. So you have to listen to me."

"Lani, I do have other things that I do besides meet with patients. I run a business with other doctors. Plus, I'm working on finishing up the new rehabilitation unit next door, in case you don't remember."

Her sister picked at her navy blue nail polish, her head lowered with full pouty lips in place. Any second tears would well and, with a quick blink, Lani would have a steady stream flowing down her cheeks—an Academy Award–winning performance. Although the theatrics didn't sway her, Erin didn't want an emotional scene in her office.

"Lani, can we do this later—like this evening? Come on over. I'll fix dinner." Erin could never say no to her sister.

"Cool. You're the best." Her sister's head popped up, a wide toothy grin now in place. She leaned over, kissed

Erin on the cheek and left, leaving a trail of heavy perfume in her wake. Her noisy, clunky jewelry jangled as the final announcement of her departure.

Erin turned back to the files on her desk. She liked spending her days in the medical world. Every day didn't come with a boring routine. She couldn't coast through a day on autopilot. The challenges she faced every day required active engagement.

She'd learned very early in her career that all problems didn't unfold into glorious outcomes. And yet, she found satisfaction in looking beyond the need to rebuild mobility or mend torn ligaments. She cared about rehabilitating the broken spirits of patients who struggled with the healing process. In this profession, she'd found her calling.

On the flipside, where her own emotions ran rampant, she viewed the terrain as foreign and too unpredictable. Her expertise with falling in or out of love could be characterized as either nonexistent or as old as the Jurassic period.

Lani, however, had earned the badge of male domination back in high school. Her sister had a repertoire of roles to play—sexy, shy or coolly detached. Inevitably, her various boyfriends would be enamored and then devastated when she grew bored of their attention.

If Erin allowed herself that slither of space to feel sorry for herself, she'd envy her sister's ability. The few men who had attracted her enough to accept their flirtation soon dropped out of her life. Too serious, they all claimed. Too strong, one in particular accused. "Doesn't know how to make a man feel like he's the man," said another. Her professional success, financially comfortable lifestyle and independence were supposed to be her so-called attractive points, but in the blink of an eye they turned into fodder for men's insecure egos.

But her sister's successes didn't come without an emotional backlash, Erin reminded herself. Every now and then, Lani did fall in love—her version of love—and then the breakups turned messy and loud. Always, she came to her big sister for the noble rescue and hand-holding mourning period until the next sucker came along. Erin wondered when her twenty-five-year-old sister would grow up. Looked like today wasn't going to be that day.

As for herself, Erin had experienced some men who'd tried to bulldoze their way into her life, but she refused to let any of them stir up the status quo. If she didn't engage in such distractions, she didn't have to worry that drama would enter her life.

Their parents had had a wonderful, long marriage before her mother died five years ago. They were the role models for greeting cards that said, "I'll love you until the end of time." Older, wiser and a lot more cynical, Erin now viewed her parents' marriage as a product of a bygone era and, quite frankly, an item for the endangered species list.

With her elderly father on a fixed income in a senior living community and the frenetic pace of Lani's lifestyle, along with her unpredictable income, Erin shouldered the responsibility as provider for the family. She didn't mind the role for it taught her how to survive on her own. Being disciplined and tenacious brought success and order to her life.

Besides, looking at Lani and all the other Lani types navigating the current social scene, she had decided that relationships relied too heavily on the heart, with inevitable one-sided sacrifice, too much compromise and blind faith in trying to change the other person's values.

None of that was for her.

Her office phone rang, calling her attention back to business.

"Dr. Wilson, Vernon Brockman, the rep from Gramercy Pharmaceutical, is on the line. He's not taking no for an answer."

"Put him through, please." She had taken this rep to task for his aggressive sales approach. Now her staff hated dealing with him. Often, she'd be called to handle him. He was lucky that a small number of the company's medicines did have fast and effective rehabilitative benefits. However, he was still an annoying gnat.

"Mr. Brockman, Dr. Wilson here. How may I assist you today?"

"Erin, my favorite doc." His nasal pitch poured the saccharin-tainted compliment over her, leaving a slimy residue. "I told them not to bother you. Hey, by the way, which professional athlete are you healing now? Can't believe I caught a glimpse of Atlanta's Chaz 'the Tiger' Owens coming out of your office the other day." His chuckle grated on her nerves. But then, he could blink and that would irk her.

Erin had had enough. "I am busy, but I definitely want to talk to you." She turned up the iciness in her tone because she wanted to be perfectly clear. "You've been pushing the Benefedra drug my way for the past month. I've read the company's report."

"Impressive, right? And more data is coming in on those early successes," he interrupted.

"Yes. But your case studies were in Russia. Not exactly the top place for clinical trials. As a matter of fact, there are a few cautionary reports from the European Medical Oversight Committee and the Harvard College of Surgeons about the dangerous addictive side effects. Something about psychotic episodes."

"There always are detractors that are working for the competition. Psychotic episodes were from patients who already had that disposition."

"And the FDA isn't even close to making a decision on the drug," she continued as if he hadn't interrupted.

"We expect that the drug will be fast-tracked."

"Then you know something I don't." The man's lack of ethics chilled her spine. She adjusted herself in the chair. He was lucky that he wasn't standing in her office, face-to-face. "I'm a Harvard graduate, and I trust my colleagues. If they advise that more clinical trials are necessary, then your company needs to follow suit. I'm not going to put my patients at risk for an experimental drug."

"The drug is beyond the experimental stage. I would think that you'd want to be on the ground floor when the big launch has happened."

"No, thanks." Erin had never been swayed by the allure of the pharmaceutical empires, large or small. As a doctor, she relied on various therapies to bring her patients back to their whole selves, or as close to that state as possible. Her job was to determine the best recourse, shift lanes if necessary or cut one route and change to another. She wasn't going to overmedicate or dispense questionable drugs.

"But, Erin," Vernon, the gnat, wheedled. Condescension coated his words. "We are giving you a great incentive. I'm not making this offer to just anyone. The potential for being one of our early clients for this drug would be a financial boon to you."

Erin grabbed her pen. The only sound in the room was the clicking of the pen. Her pupils constricted and white-hot anger surged from her core and spread through her limbs with laserlike speed. Her hand tightened around the phone to clamp the receiver closer to her ear.

"Vern, I'm only going to say this once. Do not talk to me as if I'm an idiot trolling through your used car sales lot. Do not threaten me with financial loss or dangle an incentive for a questionable product. As a matter of fact, don't ever call this office. I will be in touch with your company. And let me conclude this conversation with one more thing. I'm Dr. Wilson to you. Good day." She slammed down the phone before emitting a growl through clenched teeth. The man had made the mistake of trying to take advantage of their business relationship. She'd cut him off at the knees before she let that happen.

Erin remembered her mother's advice after she passed her medical board examinations. *Doctors could be social engineers or social piranhas.* She'd defended the medical profession with such fervor that her father had to intervene in their many heated discussions. In Erin's opinion, her colleagues all had taken the Hippocratic Oath and lived with and followed high principles that guided their every decision. She truly believed that bad doctors were a rarity. How naive could she be?

In the news, sordid members of the medical profession demonstrated their lack of ethics, the poor judgment caused by their oversize egos and voracious greed for the almighty dollar. One bad doctor was one doctor too much. No matter how many were caught, there was still another person ready to fill the dubious role. Now she understood the message her mother had insisted that she understand. She wanted to be that social engineer who worked for the betterment of the person, but also the community. If she didn't focus on that standard, she could lose her soul.

Once that downward spiral began, then she could find it too easy to violate her oath, to muddy the purpose and mission that led her to this calling and to dishonor her mother's wishes.

Her anger simmered. No idiotic pharmaceutical salesperson with the personality of a toad could tempt her with the pursuit of "dirty" money. Vern could go to hell with that mess.

And certainly, no patient *should* detract her from her calling, not even a devilishly handsome race car driver. "Marc Newton, you have just met your match. I'm not one to fall in a swoon."

Chapter 2

Erin grabbed her keys and pocketbook. She needed to calm down. After telling her staff that she was headed to lunch, she walked to the nearby parking garage to retrieve her car.

Some days her routine had no spikes to shake up her nerves. Then there were days like this that constantly had her gritting her teeth. One by one, a race car driver, her younger sister and a sleazy sales rep had come through like back-to-back microbursts, throwing off her day with their unique turbulence.

What was next? Or *who* was next?

Now that the question had been thrown out there, she feared that it might be answered in a way that would leave her ready to pull out her hair.

Behind the wheel with nowhere in mind, Erin shifted

gears, revved the engine and headed for the back roads that wound a curvy route through the farms. Being responsible was ninety-nine percent of her mind-set. Some days, like this one, that one percent of her deepest wishes had to surface like steam out of a pressure release valve.

She dreamed of escape from everything and everyone. Didn't mean that she didn't want to return. Just that she wanted to push a pause button on her life. And when she was ready, she would push Resume.

With a full gas tank, the R & B radio station on blast mode with an oldie from The Temptations and a glove compartment full of Twizzlers, Erin had all she needed for an hour-long drive to nowhere. Her pause button allowed her to leave everything behind: people and their careers, people and their emotions, people and her responsibilities.

Raleigh, North Carolina, bustled with all the trappings of a growing city, but outside the city, there remained a touch of the country that had not been developed. Family-owned farms still held fast against the push or need to sell. Single-lane roads marked the countryside, connecting one small town to the other.

Instead of dealing with the traffic congestion, crowded lunch spots and din of population, Erin sought the easy drive through the fields. Her schedule didn't allow this treat often. But she didn't miss any opportunity to play hooky.

A half hour later her cell phone buzzed with an incoming text. It was the office. Time to push the button to resume her responsibilities. Time to act like a grown-up. Erin turned down the music, closed the convertible top and headed onto the highway toward the city and her office.

The schedule for the remainder of the day had one surgery and two follow-up appointments. Since she'd invited Lani over, she couldn't stay late. That meant she'd have to bring work home and put in a few hours after Lani left to get caught up. She rubbed her stiff neck. It was going to be a long night.

Erin turned off the fire under the various pots. She'd finished cooking dinner, a task that she enjoyed but rarely had time to do. Her father, who liked his independence, insisted on cooking for himself at his apartment. With her badgering, he'd relented to having her cook for her weekly Sunday visit with him. They'd usually catch up on the week's news. More often of late they'd reminisce about earlier times.

She found a way to sneak food into his fridge by cooking larger quantities. He'd mildly protest upon the discovery of the various dishes stowed away in marked containers, but by the end of the week, the containers would be empty. Erin pretended that she didn't know the game. Her father might even sneak in a request for a certain meal or dessert as an innocent observation that he hadn't had a dish in a while and that he couldn't get it out of his thoughts.

Her sister enjoyed food. Erin had half joked that she should be a food reviewer. Lani had a knack for tasting and identifying seasonings and spices in foods. She approached eating as if the meal was the end product of a science experiment and she had to break it down to savor and enjoy. Erin didn't mind her chief role in the culinary play.

Lani paid for the heavy consumption and sweet tooth with a full figure. She exercised hard, ate lots and partied with a similar appetite. She was such a bundle of energy that any one activity, such as sitting for a meal, was too much commitment to that one task. More than likely, Lani would eat, pour out her problems, then run off. But if she wanted Erin to listen and play doctor to her love life, then they'd do it by taking an hour to sit, spend time together and enjoy a home-cooked meal.

Erin pulled out the baked chicken and placed the covered dish in the center of the table. The doorbell sounded at the same time that she carried out the sweet potato soufflé. She set it down and hastily wiped her fingers before running to the door.

"Can't believe you're actually on time." Erin greeted her sister with a hug.

"That's because Todd made sure I wasn't late."

Erin pulled out of Lani's embrace. She hadn't noticed the young man standing off to the side. He raised his hand and quickly lowered it when Lani glared at him.

"Um...please come in. I'm Erin."

"Don't worry—he's not staying," Lani retorted.

"Oh." Erin didn't necessarily want an unexpected guest. However, she wasn't going to be rude even if

Lani was going to act like a spoiled brat. "There's more than enough dinner, if you'd like to stay."

Todd shook his head.

"How is he going to stay if we're going to be talking about him?" Lani tossed out with casual indifference.

So this was the bad guy? She must be getting muddled with Lani's exes. She thought the last guy was Juan from the Dominican Republic. Not that Todd couldn't be from the D.R. with his pale white skin, sandy brown, straight hair and slate-gray eyes. But she wasn't about to open her mouth and insert foot with a name mix-up. Her best tactic at this point was to let Lani lead the way and try to cover any potholes her sister created with her lack of diplomacy.

Todd, on the other hand, stayed where he was in the living room. Unlike Lani's big dramatic flair with her arms and body language, he stayed cool, his expression successfully blank. Young and stoic. Quite a combination, she thought.

"Todd, you can go. Shoo." Lani flicked her hands, bracelets clanging.

Todd nodded and left.

Erin waited until the door clicked shut. "You are a piece of work."

"What's the problem? I was up front. I told him that I needed to talk to my sister. You invited me. He wanted to drive."

"Wash up." Erin finished bringing the food and dishes to the table. "I can't wait to hear this story. And what happened to Juan?"

"Juan?" Lani stepped into the half bath in the hall-way. She shouted from the room, "He went back to the D.R. Wanted me to go with him. Not happening." She came out drying her hands on her pants. "Plus I think he was married."

Erin could only stare at her sister's cavalier manner toward all her relationships, even theirs. She'd like to think that Lani had suddenly become callous, but no, they had always been distinctly on different paths on the personal aspects of their lives.

"And Todd?"

Lani shrugged. "He wants to marry me."

Erin dropped the carving knife with a clatter. She took a seat and waited for Lani to sit opposite her.

After a few seconds of silence, Erin bravely asked, "Why?"

"Why would he want to marry me?" Lani's eyebrow cocked to match the incredulity of her sister's question.

Erin nodded. She felt that she had a stable job—thriving if you took a look at her income statement. She had a house, small but elegantly furnished. She had a convertible, with no accidents, not even a moving vio-lation on her license. She hadn't slept with enough men to make up a football team, not that she was judging. But darn it, her little sister, who could play the evil step-sister in any version of Cinderella, kept getting these guys who wanted to be around her caustic personality.

"They want me for the sex."

Erin choked on the soda she'd just sipped. Now that was an element that she hadn't checked off against her sister. Her own nether parts hadn't been touched by a man in a long time. By her sex toys—oh, maybe a month ago. She was too busy to think about such matters. There was a plus side to her drought, though. She could focus on work and put in long hours so that she was too tired to miss an hour of good sex.

"Todd wants to get engaged and marry next year. I don't do long courtships. But to be tied down to one man is so old-school."

"Our parents did it—happily for thirty-five years." Erin's irritation reared. "Don't knock it."

"Todd is sweet. But too wholesome. Kinda creepy."

"Going the straight and narrow has its rewards. You know what to expect. You can trust. You can look forward to a future on your terms."

"Boring!" Lani filled her mouth with chicken. Her cheek bulged while she tapped the table with her fork handle. "You're supposed to be talking me out of this."

"I'm not trying to talk you out of or into anything. Lani, you always tell me to be honest with you. So…I don't think you're mature enough to handle any kind of a relationship. And I'm feeling sorry for Todd. I want to tell him to run."

Lani howled in full protest. "What the heck? Were you saving all that up to dump on me when I'm down?"

"No need to get indignant." Erin shoved aside her plate. Watching Lani turn into a screaming witch wasn't ever pretty. But enough was enough. After all, she had said that she wanted logic and unemotional feedback.

"You called me immature? I've got a paralegal

job, an efficiency apartment and a little bit of money. Haven't needed to borrow any money from you."

"I think they call them gifts when there is no repayment in sight." Erin sniffed at Lani's claims.

"You always have to fling your success in my face. Not everyone is an overachiever in every tiny part of her life. Not everyone feels that having fun is a sin. Not everyone thinks about work 24/7. That's called no life. I'd say that's a form of immaturity." Lani snapped her fingers. "I got it. You're stagnant."

"I'm not the one with issues." Erin's temper rose. "I'm not the one who needs advice—not with my profession or my life and certainly not about any man."

"That's because you don't need advice when you've done nothing to warrant it." Lani stood up, pushing back the chair. "You've always got to make this about you. This is about Todd and me. Marriage. Babies."

"Please tell me you're not—" Erin held her breath.

"Of course not. I'm just sayin'."

Erin rubbed her forehead, trying to erase the band of tension that tightened with a dull ache. Guilt prickled and poked at her conscience for snapping at Lani. Why did she frequently allow Lani to get under her skin?

As close as their relationship was, they knew how to tap-dance on each other's insecurities with dogged intensity. Afterward, the impact left wounds of various sizes to be healed. Her wounds were kept buried so deep that she'd forget they existed until something rolled back the covering from her hiding place.

If their mother was alive, she'd have reproached

them for their catty behavior. She'd have turned an even fiercer eye on Erin for being twenty-seven and acting like a jealous teen. Her mom was not the type to encourage family feuds.

"Lani, have a seat. Look, I want to help you." Erin reached over the table and placed her hand over her sister's. "You're my sweet Candy Lane." She tenderly squeezed Lani's hand. "Let's talk, lil' sis. I'm listening."

By the time Lani had left, Erin wanted to open the bottle of wine that she'd received in a gift basket. Working through Lani's issues required some finesse so that her sister could learn how to analyze and solve her own problems. Todd was a silent figure in all of this because she didn't know his take on anything; she had to rely on Lani's point of view to focus on her and not try to change Todd.

The final verdict that night rolled out with Lani not accepting Todd's proposal—just yet. Instead they would take the time to court and become friends. Then they could revisit the proposal at some later date. All that sounded fine to Lani, except she wanted specific insertions in the timeline for the great sex to be had with Todd.

Erin decided that particular call for action crossed the line beyond her responsibility as big sister. All she could do was kiss the top of Lani's head and send her on her way with Todd, who was summoned to play chauffeur for the ride home.

Tired, but knowing that she had several work-related

tasks to complete, she made herself a cup of coffee to blast the early signs of sleepiness. With her laptop in front of her, she logged into her email system. The list of unread emails was lengthy, but an email from Newton Enterprises made her sit up.

She opened the email and read: Dr. Wilson, we received your report on Marc Newton. Thank you for your speedy response. However, we are concerned with your draft recommendation. Please contact us at your earliest convenience.

Draft? There was nothing in her report that was in draft form. What exactly did they want to discuss?

Marc Newton shouldn't be driving until he healed and had another checkup. He didn't like the news, but she wasn't budging. Now he'd pulled out his big guns to do battle with her. She cracked her knuckles and sat back with a grin. "Bring it, Marc Newton."

Marc stood in the middle of the auto shop. His small staff formed a semicircle in front of him and waited to be addressed. At the beginning of each week, he started the morning with a pep talk. He was the head of this company, but each person on the floor looking back at him had an important role in the company's success. What had started nine years ago in a small warehouse had grown into a strong company that was his life's blood.

"Ladies and gentlemen, we've got an upcoming race that will set the tone for the next season. Therefore, we can't sit on our laurels. Each of you is an important element to having a successful team. I will do my part, too. We're going to get over this hurdle with my medical stuff. Nothing is going to keep me down."

A small cheer erupted. Marc noted that the enthusiasm wasn't as robust as the same time last year—or any other year. Hard times stood in the doorway of his company, ready to barge in and run him over. Being a double failure settled in his gut like a lead weight, as a businessman and as a driver.

"We've got new deals with suppliers. Two more sponsors have signed on. I'll be catching up with the department heads immediately after this meeting. Well, that's it." He clapped his hands and was glad to hear a livelier cheer from his staff. Morale was on the agenda for discussion with the managers.

The next meeting was held in his office with his small number of supervisors. He sat on the edge of his desk, deliberately eliminating the formality of his position. He pushed up his sleeves and waited for everyone to get seated and comfortable.

"Good speech, boss."

"Thanks, Lionel. Not sure I removed the doubts, but I need folks to hang in there. It's not too early to think about next season. Sponsors aren't guaranteed. Our early wins haven't given us much cushion."

"You're worrying too much. They—we—are all behind you," Lionel responded.

Marc had hired Lionel as his first employee. Nine years ago the older man had moved from California with his girlfriend and her two children. At the time,

Lionel desperately needed a job. Marc went out on a limb and hired him, although his only job experience was as an auto mechanic. He'd never regretted the decision. Lionel worked hard and showed initiative to dive into the auto racing industry. Now his manager, Lionel had also served as a spotter, a key trusted position on the race team.

"Behind me? Some days, I need you right beside me or even in front to help me along," Marc confessed.

"Always," Lionel affirmed, along with the others.

"Martha, what's up with marketing?"

"You keep turning down requests." Martha shook her head. Her mouth turned down, displaying her annoyance. He didn't miss the exaggerated eye roll.

"I don't want to do interviews or be on goofy commercials." Marc worked hard to keep people out of his private life.

"Not even a reality show? Would bring in money."

"And distractions. We can't afford any delays or anyone nosing around in our lives. We need to focus and plan ahead."

Martha pushed. "Before you make any hasty decisions, just think about it."

Marc hated dealing with the media and their probing questions that inevitably led to his private life. Certain parts of his life—the secret painful memories, his agonizing loss—need never surface under public scrutiny. It took a lot of effort to secure his privacy. Reporters didn't care to linger on what it took to be a driver, his journey, the legacy he wanted to create. Instead they wanted him to perform on cue like a trained animal, posing and talking about nonsense and selling his soul for men's cologne.

"Are you racing in two weeks?" Lionel asked.

Marc nodded. "Why wouldn't I be?"

"Just wondered. I…well, I dunno—"

Marc held his counsel on the possibility that he couldn't race. He wasn't going to give voice to his fears. Plus, thinking about it only brought the annoying doctor to mind.

"On another note," Tony, his crew chief, interjected, "I've heard that John Lewis isn't happy with his team. He might be looking for a new home to call his own."

"Really?" Marc resisted being too interested before he got all the facts. Dealing with his own health issues had distracted him from paying attention to what was happening behind the scenes in the racing community. Drivers, teams and crew or pit chiefs shifted each season to create new winning teams or to breathe life into an old team.

"We have talked about recruiting." The crew chief sounded eager.

"But John is a pain. There is a reason why he's possibly moving on to his second team," Lionel interjected.

"Can't deny that he's a good driver. He's got the edge. Isn't afraid to take risks. He's hungry," Martha added.

Marc listened to Martha's assessment of Lewis. His marketing guru knew what she was talking about, but there was also an open admiration for the man.

"I guess you're suggesting that someone talk to him," Marc said.

They all looked at him.

Marc crossed his arms. "We'll see." John would be an asset but would be high maintenance from the beginning. There were some others he'd approach first.

In quick order, his supervisors provided a summary of major activity happening within their departments. Marc followed up with a few questions. Overall, he was satisfied with operations. Now it was time to get back to his personal situation—being able to race in two weeks.

He stood. His legs almost buckled. A wave of dizziness hit as if someone held his head in a tight grasp and shook it a couple times. He gritted his teeth, determined to push away the nausea.

"Okay, boss?" Lionel paused in his side conversation with Martha.

"Yeah. Must have been the egg sandwich from this morning," he lied. Coffee had been his only meal. He tapped his stomach for emphasis.

"I have some antacids in my desk," his crew chief said as he exited the office.

Marc didn't protest. Cold sweat had broken out on his forehead. This could not be happening. He blinked his eyes to see if the condition lessened. On a good note, at least the sensation didn't get worse. He walked over to his coffeemaker and poured a cup. Without dressing it up with cream or sugar, he drank the coffee, bracing himself against the bold taste. When everything failed, coffee was his medicine of choice.

Marc accepted the antacids and then shooed everyone out of his office. The minute the door closed, he walked around the desk and sat heavily in the chair. The muscles supporting his neck wound tight like corded rope pulling up at his shoulders. Tension didn't ease as the muscles continued to twist into the back of his head. His head still felt as if it had been locked in an unyielding vise.

Maybe he was coming down with a sinus infection. The change in the weather certainly did come with its range of allergens. He prayed that he'd feel better quickly.

He closed his eyes against the fluorescent glare of the overhead light. Nursing injuries after a race wasn't new. The reality came with the job. However, his car did flip after being clipped by another aggressive driver, and his seat belt had snapped loose. Regardless, he had to push aside the grumblings from his body and move on. Car racing and injuries were an inevitable partnership.

A knock on his door jarred his attempt to empty his mind for a chance to relax. He tried to ignore this latest assault to his nerves. His staff knew that if he didn't respond, it was a sign to leave him alone. Truthfully, he didn't expect to win the warm and fuzzy award from them. But he did show remorse for his temper with more meaningful ways like bonuses and days off.

"Now that's a good reason for not answering my knock."

"Dr. Wilson?" Marc blinked twice to see if his unsettling head affected his vision. Nope. The doctor stood

Racing Hearts

near the door looking down her nose at him. The ponytail she'd last worn had given way to a simple part in the middle with her hair loose on either side of her face, flowing to her shoulders.

"You don't look well." Dr. Wilson crossed the room and walked behind his desk, right up to his chair. She reached toward him.

Marc backed away. He didn't care if she creased her forehead with a million frowns. "You're on my turf."

"And what's that supposed to mean to me?" She raised her hand again toward him. This time he didn't pull away. Gently she laid the back of her hand against his forehead.

"I don't plan to undergo another examination," he protested.

"You could make things easier and let me check you over or pass out and head to the hospital in an ambulance." She checked his pulse next.

"I'm fine now." His head had cleared.

"Your pulse is slightly raised. What have you been doing?"

"I was giving my team a pep talk," Marc retorted.

"Hmm."

"Then you walked in."

"Hmm."

"Come to deliver more bad news?" He eyed her warily.

"Well, that would depend." Once the doctor was done looking into his eyes and feeling his lymph nodes, she moved in front of the desk. "Your investors failed in their attempt to overturn my decision about your case." She smiled, more like displayed an evil grin. "Looks like I will now be pressured to making sure you get into tip-top shape so you can earn your keep. That's the reason that I came. I wanted to deliver my message in person."

Marc groaned. He didn't care if her delicate feelings got hurt. This situation just plain sucked. He only wished that his pulse would stop spiking as if he was racing by foot around the track. Like he kept telling himself, she wasn't his type.

Too sensible.

Too stubborn.

She removed her glasses, resting the tip of the handle against her full glossy lips. Her gaze narrowed, lips tightened at his visual trespass. Maybe he shouldn't have stared at her mouth.

Too darn sexy.

He meant *too* safe. She had the girl-next-door demeanor. The girl next door who also happened to be brilliant, confident and compellingly attractive.

Chapter 3

Erin pulled away from Marc and dropped her hands to her side. Could he possibly sense the effect of her attraction to him flooding her system? If he did, then his cool cockiness reminded her to take a mental step back. Even with his symptoms, he still had a powerful aura. His eyes shifted from her face and slid lazily along the contours of her body before he readjusted his steady gaze on her face. Her body's traitorous response sent a surge of heat that spiked and exploded through her body. She wanted to clamp her hands on her cheeks to hide her blush.

Blushing wasn't a frequent occurrence given the fact that she had no one in her life to make her pulse race. Maybe she was out of practice and a little weak against Marc's empty flirtation. She hadn't spent eight years getting her degree and license to be reduced to a horny idiot in front of a gorgeous patient.

Erin pulled out her car keys and swung her pocketbook over her shoulder. "I'm ready to drive you to the hospital for tests."

"I only have a pinched nerve."

"Maybe."

"Likely." He reached for the phone while staring at her. Only when he needed to dial did he shift his gaze. He spoke briefly and then hung up. "A car is available to take us to the hospital. *My* doctor will meet us there."

Erin bristled. Now she'd have two stubborn men fighting her decision.

"Any problems with that?"

She shook her head. "Let's go. The sooner we can figure out the problem, the better."

Marc stood and had to grip the edge of the desk. His fingernails turned white from the pressure to keep himself upright.

"Would you like me to ask one of your staff to assist you to the car?" She walked toward the door. "Or I'd be happy to offer my arm for support."

A flash of anger illuminated his eyes, and his mouth hardened. He muttered under his breath. Without responding, he straightened up and walked out. His brow furrowed as he tried to push away the headache he nursed.

"Are you coming?" he mumbled over his shoulder.

"Just giving you enough room to fall backward."

"Some doctor you are," Marc continued to mumble.

"Yeah, I'm lousy like that—caring about my patients, dispensing advice, even personally escorting them to hospitals."

"You don't have to come," Marc said.

"Oh, but I do. I so want to say 'I told you so.'"

He headed out the door to the waiting car. Before he got in, he cocked his head. "Do you have siblings?"

"A sister. Younger."

"Hmm. That explains a lot."

Erin lightly pushed him into the car. She'd never manhandled a patient before, but somehow, Marc had a knack for squirming under her skin. Whatever he had to say, she wasn't interested to hear. She knew all the stupid firstborn statistics. Since college, she'd heard that over half of U.S. presidents were firstborns. Even her father had jumped on the bandwagon to convince her throughout her childhood that she was a natural leader.

Maybe knowing the traits about being reliable, conscientious and a perfectionist caused her to be a doormat for her sister's shenanigans. She was honest enough to know that she had a slight superiority complex. Well, she blamed the statistics for convincing her that she was a favorable asset to have on anyone's team.

"How far is the hospital?" Marc asked. The silence in the car grew heavy and uncomfortable.

"Ten minutes," the driver responded.

She glanced over at Marc. Now he laid his head to the side with his eyes closed. She leaned a little closer to inspect.

"I'm still breathing."

"You look as if you're in pain."

"Trying to block your perfume."

Erin instinctively sniffed her wrists where she had touched a dab of scent. "Sorry." She pulled out a hand wipe.

"It's not offensive." He breathed deeply and then opened his eyes to half slits. His mouth offered a small smile. "The fragrance has a delicate note that will sear into my memory even after you're gone."

"It's my favorite." She didn't know if she should still wipe her wrists. Having any part of her seared into Marc's memory stirred a mysterious element deep within that sluggishly awoke from its dormancy.

The Doctor's Hospital outside of Morristown was smaller than most community hospitals, but she knew that she could guarantee Marc's privacy. Not that he'd rely on her for those services. Already, three members of his inner circle were pulling into the lot in their cars.

They herded him into the E.R. wing without a glance at her. Erin followed. She had no desire to have a contest with them over their boss, though they did act as if she might kidnap him. She may not know their world, but she did know hers. Judging from Marc's symptoms, she was fairly certain that she was not being overly cautious.

The admitting nurse processed the paperwork in no time. Almost immediately he was escorted through the heavy automatic doors that swung open and closed before being locked into place.

The entourage, made up of the three-person inner circle and her, as the outsider, was barred entry. Now the waiting would begin. Tests and results could take hours. The E.R. didn't operate with the primary purpose of alleviating the family's and friends' inconvenience.

"Has anyone contacted a relative?" Erin asked the group in general. She knew nothing about Marc. He was a race car hero to many, but she didn't follow the sport, much less its icons. As a result much of the buzz was lost on her. That didn't mean that she wouldn't take the opportunity to learn more about him—directly from the source in the next couple of weeks.

The woman in the group answered, "His dad knows. He'll be here shortly."

"That's it?" Erin asked with open curiosity. No way that Mr. I'm-Too-Sexy didn't have a female companion reclining on a chaise lounge somewhere. Someone, other than Dad, had to be worried. No way did they share the lack of a special someone in their lives.

"That's it," one of the men replied with more than a touch of frost in his attitude. He turned his back and continued his conversation with the other man and woman. Erin recalled hearing Marc call him Lionel.

"I'm not the enemy," she muttered at their united front to freeze her out. Instead of standing in the waiting area like a lonely island, she opted to get a coffee. The polite thing would be to ask if the others wanted anything. But she wasn't feeling polite. And she certainly wasn't feeling included.

She turned to leave the area and bumped into a tall, older gentleman. He grabbed her by the arms to steady her with an apology underscored by a quick laugh.

"I should be looking where I'm going." Erin tried to explain her goof.

"No worries. I'm the one rushing through the hall. Looking for my son."

Erin studied the face. Familiar features were aimed at her: the strong slope of his forehead, angular jawline, the casual tilt of his head. Recognition clicked into place.

"Are you Marc's dad?"

He nodded. "Wallace Newton."

"Erin Wilson. His doctor. Well, not his primary doctor. Orthopedist."

"Did he suffer another injury?"

"Ah, no. I'm his orthopedist who was hired after the last accident. I was visiting him today in his office. He looked a little worn around the edges. I'm sure that he's still feeling a bit achy, which is normal after the initial accident." She pointed her thumb toward the E.R. doors. "They are running a few tests at my request."

"Good."

"Mr. Newton, hi, good to see you." Lionel entered Erin's space, planting himself between Wallace and her. "I don't expect anything to come of this." His tone clearly indicated that he wasn't in support of her actions.

"Better safe." Mr. Newton looked at her and nodded.

"Of course. Although Marc wasn't keen on the tests." Lionel sounded like a snitch.

The older Newton straightened his posture. "When Marc becomes a medical doctor then he'll be worth listening to about his health." His irritation toward Lionel was open for all to see.

"Can I get you a cup of coffee?" Lionel asked, now clearly trying to make amends.

"Erin?" Wallace stepped to the side to bypass Lionel's deliberate block.

"Actually, I was heading to the cafeteria for coffee and a sandwich. I figured it'll take some time before we hear any news."

"I'll go with you, then. Lionel, nice seeing you. Just buzz me when you hear something."

"The doctor will notify me." Erin held up her pager. She didn't have to play at Lionel's game, but maybe it was the firstborn instincts kicking in to show off that she also had connections.

"That's settled. Let's go. Call me Wallace, by the way."

"Okay, Wallace, let's beat the lunch crowd."

Erin strolled next to the older Newton. Although he walked with a slow gait, his long legs created wide strides that made her shorter legs have to work harder. Unlike his son's radioactive charisma, Wallace exuded a fun, relaxed vibe that quickly set her nerves at ease.

They navigated the many halls and elevators to the cafeteria on the third floor. The noon crowd wasn't due for another thirty minutes. From the hub of activity in the expansive room, several patrons had used her logic and come early.

"You go ahead and get your food. I'll grab a table." Wallace headed off to one of the small booths among the sea of stand-alone tables and chairs. He waved away her protests.

"What if I picked up something for you?" Erin offered.

"I don't have a clue what I'm in the mood for. I'll get something next."

Erin nodded and headed to the display table of food. As quickly as possible, she gathered her lunch and headed for the seat.

Wallace didn't take long. He returned with his hands full of yogurt, fruit and a bottle of water. Erin looked forward to chatting with him. His personality was friendly and welcoming. Maybe she'd get some tidbits on his son.

"Erin, how did you manage to convince Marc to take more tests?"

"I wish that I could say I convinced him." Erin shook her head. "I had to threaten him. Plus I have to give my opinion on when he's ready to drive."

"That couldn't have put you on his good side. These days, I don't think he has a side other than worrying and obsessing about his company. He needs a life beyond cars." Using his plastic spoon to emphasize his point, he continued, "I hope you can manage to insert that into the therapy. Might help him to have a good mood every now again. He's killing himself being owner and driver." He sighed. "Sorry, I'm rambling on."

Erin wanted to agree, but stayed silent. This tract sounded like a common theme of discontent between father and son. She wanted to avoid such conflict. In a few months, her contract with his sponsors would be up. She'd close the file on Marc Newton and return to her practice minus him.

"What keeps you busy besides my son?"

"I have a new practice with a few doctors. Busy is an understatement."

"Don't let it take over what's important to you."

Erin nodded. In her opinion, she covered all the things that were important. If it didn't fit, then she couldn't classify it as important.

"Anyone special? Yes, I'm nosy." He laughed.

"Not at the moment." She didn't laugh. Now she felt defensive.

"A pretty woman like you? I can't believe that. I suppose men are intimidated by your profession." He snorted his disgust. "Those men you definitely don't need to deal with. Keep morons out of your life."

"I don't have the time to date. So I won't know the reason. I'm not missing out on anything." Erin shrugged and offered no further insight. Although easygoing, Wallace couldn't be her confidant. She finished her last bite of sandwich and balled up the paper. The motion matched what she'd done with her love life—rolled it up and tossed it aside.

Her pager beeped, and they both jumped.

Erin called the number and listened to the doctor relay the details. "Looks like they are all done. He's ready to go home. They want us to meet them in one of the offices near the waiting area."

Wallace was already on his feet. He'd cleared their trash. "I'm ready."

She wished that she could erase the worried frown with a comforting diagnosis, but she hadn't been told the results. This time, she took the lead and hurried through the halls.

She entered the crowded office. Marc was seated in one of two chairs for visitors. The inner circle stood nearby, hovering over their leader. Erin gestured to the other chair for Wallace.

"No need. I'll stand. I'm only interested in what the doctor has to say."

"Dad, they didn't have to call you." Marc turned a dark stare at his staff. They mumbled, but no one spoke up to admit to calling his father.

"I'm sure that he'd have been more worried if word had gotten out that you were in the hospital," Erin ventured.

"Doc, let's hear the news," Marc prompted the doctor. He looked pleased, as if he already knew the news and it contradicted what she'd thought.

"Well, Marc will be driving for as long as he wants. His tests didn't come back with anything significantly wrong. He needs to rest a little more, but he can start working on the muscle tear at the back of his neck. That's going to take some time to heal. Driving will aggravate it."

"Is there any way to speed up the process? Can't afford to sit on my laurels." Marc rubbed his shoulder.

"Therapy. And that may not be enough, but it's better than nothing. I definitely wouldn't advise skipping any therapeutic workout." He looked over to Erin. "She is one of the best doctors out there. I suggest you listen to her." He looked at his watch. "I've got to get going unless you have any further questions."

Erin appreciated Dr. Singh's ringing endorsement. Not that Marc or his team would care. But she respected her mentor, and his confidence boosted her. She looked over to Marc, who now turned his attention to her as if she'd just entered the room.

"When is the next race?" Wallace asked.

"In a week." Lionel spoke up. "Can you, not your staff, help with his therapy?" he asked Erin.

"I'm not coming to the hospital every day." Marc stated emphatically, interrupting before she could reply. "You can't contain that news. Besides I have a lot of work to do in the house."

"Then have her come to the house," Lionel said.

"Is anyone going to ask if I have the availability? I do have a practice…. A thriving one, I might add." Erin bristled under their high-handed behavior. Even though she had planned to work with Marc, she didn't care for their presumption. Who knew working for the rich and famous would reduce her to being treated like a second-class citizen?

Wallace stepped forward. "If I may interject before any of you insult this woman any further. Marc, you plan to race in the next two weeks. It sounds like you can do so, but with a lot of pain. I know you're hardheaded, but this is taking your stubbornness to an extreme." Wallace turned his attention to the team. "Gentlemen, your solution is standing in front of you." He swept his arm out toward Erin.

She wanted to hug this man.

"Now I suggest you ask nicely. If I were in her shoes, I wouldn't be bothered with the lot of you."

The team muttered among themselves until Lionel emerged as the spokesperson. His chest puffed up a bit, and his nervous gestures resembled a cautious bird testing the safety of the area. The man still hadn't made eye contact with her. Was working with a woman that distasteful? Maybe he was shy? Or maybe he was just a flaming idiot.

Erin refused to make it any easier for them. She gathered up her pocketbook. With a nod to Dr. Singh, who had hung around, she turned her attention to the mixed bag of men and one woman. "I have to get back to work. You can check with my staff for my schedule. I made the offer to assist earlier, and when Marc refused, I then continued filling my calendar. However, I will do my best to find you someone on my staff to take care of you." She tilted up her chin and exited the room.

Small victories had to be celebrated just as much as the big ones. Telling them where to shove their apology felt good.

"Dr. Wilson." Wallace hurried after her. "Wait. I must say job well done in there. Now they all look confused. You know, it surprises me that they manage to have a successful race car business. Maybe that's all their egos can handle." His expression turned serious.

"But I will ask here on the side, out of earshot, that you work with Marc, please. I'm confident that you can get him on the mend."

"Wallace, I had no intention of letting Marc get out of my grasp." She held up her hand and closed her fist tightly for emphasis. "I'm no pushover."

He shook her hand, still laughing. "I will have to drop in to see you at work. You're amazing."

"My office will always be open to you. I look forward to seeing you again. And I look forward to working with your son. Somehow, though, I don't think he'll reciprocate those sentiments."

Chapter 4

Marc stormed through the next two days with a fiery temper that had everyone scattering. The media had already started talking about his potential retirement. How fickle their tastes were. In a flash, he would be yesterday's news.

The other teams barely contained their satisfaction that he may be sidelined. They called him the Maverick not as a compliment, but as an upstart who had managed to push into their sanctum. He'd done it with all the passion and focus of a man having something to prove, but with equal fervor he had nothing to lose.

No one, not even his father, knew why he pushed himself. How could they understand the guilt that threatened to stifle him on a daily basis? No matter how many times he said, I'm sorry. No matter how he raged that life could be coldhearted. Nothing could turn back time to give him a few more precious seconds, hours, years with his brother.

His twin had died at eight years old from leukemia. While he could rationalize things as an adult, there was still a part of him locked in that childhood phase, shouting that it wasn't fair. Why did Matt die, but he survived? Why did he have to say goodbye at eight years old?

Their special bond as twins intertwined with their emotions, thoughts, even how they communicated with each other without saying a word. Witnessing this malevolent force suck out the vibrancy from his brother until he was a fragile shell of a boy had torn a hole in his heart. The wound healed with a thickened shield against anything that dared to take residence in his heart. He tried to be rational, but waiting for bad things to happen in life usually nestled in his core.

On the day of his twin's death, he'd made a vow. Matt's short life wouldn't be in vain. Every second of his day was spent in dedication to his brother. He'd built this company in his memory.

That dogged determination came with a heavy price. Only when Marc was in the car behind the wheel pushing the vehicle and his body to extraordinary limits did he feel at peace. When he raced, he didn't care about the what-ifs. Success was all that mattered.

Nothing was too much to pay for what he still had to accomplish. If that meant that he had to subject himself to Erin's medicinal touch, then so be it. But she had better not stand between him and what he had to do.

"Lionel, I'm heading out."

"Anything you need?"

"Nah. Heading to Dr. Wilson to smooth out things."

"Good luck. She's a real ice queen."

Marc stared hard at Lionel. He might think she was a hard-ass, but he didn't appreciate anyone on his team referring to her in that fashion. Not that he felt the need to protect her. She had a stiffer backbone than most people he'd encountered.

He grabbed his jacket with one destination in mind.

Marc sat in Erin's office, where he'd been ushered and advised that she'd be in to see him in a few minutes. He'd spent time in the examination room, but never in her office. A quick survey revealed what he'd already suspected. Dr. Wilson was a neat freak.

He reached over to her desk and nudged a neatly stacked ornament set askew. The geometric shapes lay in a heap. He felt much better and leaned back in his chair satisfied with himself.

"Now that you've disarranged my desk, what can I do for you?"

Marc jumped at the sound of Erin's cool castigation. Not a good way to start things off, although he felt no remorse. But he could pretend. He leaned over and re-adjusted the ornament to its original pose.

"All fixed." He grinned.

"Hmm." She didn't sit behind her desk. Instead, she sat at the edge of the desk and folded her arms.

"I came to offer an olive branch," Marc said.

"Listening."

"Straight up, I'm going to race in the next two weeks. I need my body in the best shape possible. Will you please be available?" He didn't expect to have to wait for her response. As a matter of fact, he assumed she'd jump at the chance.

Instead she kept her cool welcome at the chilled level. Her face expressed nothing. Well, if he was going to be nitpicky with his observation, her raised eyebrow earned his irritation.

"I told your team that I'd make someone available."

"Yeah, I got that. Not acceptable."

"Oh, really?" She now stood, brown eyes narrowed to an angry squint.

Marc sighed. "Look, I don't want the second best in your practice." He tried a different tactic. "I'll be sure to talk about your healing hands every chance I get."

Erin sniffed. "Are you now going to throw dollar bills at me? Sounds like that's your method of negotiating."

Marc just couldn't get things right between Erin and him. Any other time he wouldn't care. Really, when did he have to work this hard to get a woman to do what he wanted? That sordid ease drew his boredom faster than they could have imagined.

But he liked a challenge.

Marc pushed. "How can I get you to change your mind?"

"By not treating me as if I'm one of your hanger-on girls."

Marc didn't realize that his clumsy attempts had cheapened her sensibilities. Wow! He wasn't any better than his men or the other men on the track that talked trash about the female drivers or about the women who hung around long after the crowds dispersed to be invited into the trailers.

"You know you can hire a physical therapist and get the results without dealing with me," Erin offered.

"I know. But I don't want anyone else." He kept his gaze lowered to his hands. Safer. The minute he thought about who he wanted, her face came to mind. Then he had to look at her—and not in a patient-to-doctor way.

"I have Monday, Tuesday and Thursday available. You may stop in at ten. The workout will only be an hour."

"What about the other days?"

"I'll have the physician assistant work on you in my stead."

"Okay." Three days in her care was better than nothing. It would give him time to lengthen this tentative thaw between them and guarantee his release to race. He hadn't changed his mind about winning her over.

Erin finally walked behind her desk to take a seat. Battling with Marc did cause a sensory overload. Standing so close to his sexy body did funny things to her knees, hence having to lean against the desk for support. She had to will herself to remain still and take on the persona of the coolheaded doctor in charge. Being close to him was like standing too close to the sun.

"Is there anything else I can do for you?" Erin asked, uncomfortable with the lull in the discussion.

"Yes. I'd like to take you out for dinner sometime."

"The olive branch was sufficient." Erin didn't want to be tested with crossing the line. She'd fail, no doubt about that.

"Is being in my company unpleasant? Do I want to hear the answer?"

Erin paused. She didn't expect him to care what she thought about him. "No, not unpleasant." Not even close to being unpleasant. He would never know.

"You do eat lunch?" He looked at his watch. "'Cause it's lunchtime."

"As a matter of fact, I usually skip lunch. But I'll give you thirty minutes of my time."

They walked over to the small coffee shop across the street. He'd pulled on his shades and wore a baseball cap. She noticed that he tensed if anyone stared for more than a few seconds or did a double take. She couldn't imagine living a life constantly on guard against people zeroing in on her. Life in a fishbowl was how she thought of it.

Once they ordered and received their respective cups of coffee, they headed to a table next to an expansive window allowing in natural light. The place seemed to be a popular hangout for the lunch crowd. Navy blue and black suits heavily populated the patrons' wardrobes.

The aroma of fresh bread tantalized her appetite. She

worked hard to resist following the scent to the sandwich prep area to order a favorite of hers—ham and cheese on an Italian roll. This wasn't a normal lunch date. This was Marc trying to work his way into her good graces. She had to stay mentally nimble to outwit any strategy to win her over by underhanded means like sexy flirtatious banter and come-hither looks.

"Your father is a dear." She opened up the conversation on neutral ground.

Marc nodded. "He's my biggest supporter. My mom is, too. They're divorced though. She lives in Europe, moves around quite a bit."

Erin offered, "My biggest supporters are my father and younger sister. Mom died several years ago. I needed the support from my dad and sister while I was going to university. Otherwise, I wouldn't have finished my degree."

"The practice is your life?"

"Basically." She sipped her coffee. "And your company?"

"Everything to me."

Erin set down her cup. She had to ask the question that had been nagging her ever since she was hired to attend to Marc. "Why? Why risk your life to drive at warp speed?"

"It's what all young boys love to do. The difference is that I took it into adulthood. Maybe I'm a child at heart."

Erin nodded. Although his words had a lighter feel, there was a shadow that crossed his countenance. What lay beneath that gruff, brooding exterior? Delving past the ego held an exciting thrill that spoke to her curiosity. Marc Newton had so many layers that she suspected they effectively hid the real man at the core.

"What do you risk on a daily basis?" he asked her.

Erin stared down into the cup. Her coffee had cooled, but she kept the cup clutched in her hands. Otherwise, she'd be clicking her pen.

Nothing in her life was a risk. She'd planned every inch of it, planning for various outcomes to avoid surprises.

No, risk didn't motivate her. As a child, living with her mother's rheumatoid arthritis and seeing the devastation of the illness scared her. By the time she attended college, she used that fear to set her on a path in the medical profession. Maybe she was too idealistic, but she wanted to dedicate her service to helping others with debilitating diseases.

Her mother's suffering not only nurtured her determination, but it pulled the family together. Her dad's spirit had dissolved under the emotional strain. His love for her mother couldn't overcome her illness. Erin couldn't imagine the depth of hurt and despair when a soul mate had to live a life of extreme pain.

She didn't think that she had the strength to cope. She greatly admired and respected the families she'd met through her practice. It was one thing to be a health care provider, but quite another to be the supportive pillar for that ailing person.

"I don't take risks." Erin partially shared her

thoughts. "I think it's time to be heading back. And I'll see you on Monday."

"How about before then? Say, Saturday? Sunday?"

Now that was totally unexpected. Those eyes, brown, warm, inviting, had the power to solicit her body in a strange, exhilarating way that promised new heights. With every action, there was a reaction. That would explain why her mouth slowly opened and she responded, "Saturday."

"Good. I'll pick you up."

"What will we do?"

Marc smiled. "Not sure, but it will be memorable. By the way, are you afraid of heights?"

Erin narrowed her gaze. "No. I even like roller coasters. Now you've got me thinking." She shared her address.

Her heartbeat thudded against her chest. Her breath quickened. She recognized the symptoms of a panic attack—racing heart, cold sweat, dizziness and the desire to flee.

Options. Must consider options if she was really going through with this—whatever *this* was.

Maybe if she didn't think of this quick interlude as a date, she could act as if she had good sense.

"Is this a date?" Erin decided to get an official answer.

"I'm calling it that."

A date! She needed wiggle room before definitively using that word. Everyone knows that one date leads to another, one kiss leads to another, a touch on the arm leads to a moment in the bed. How to plan for the consequences?

Well, she might need her hair touched up. An inch of new growth already showed at her roots. Lani could assist with that since she had no time to get to a hairdresser. Clothes—she didn't have time to shop. A kiss from him? Oh, man, that was like waving chocolates under her nose. Sex with him! Her mind ran with the thought, but the no-nonsense part of her, with all the rules of behavior, lessons handed down from mother and grandmother and her father's disapproving frown, told her to stop the madness.

Erin stood in front of Lani for the fifth time. So far, her sister had expressed her dislike for each outfit with a litany of crude comments.

"Keep this up and I'll change my mind," Erin threatened. Any excuse to get a rain check would do.

"You've got less than an hour. Why are your clothes so dreadful? When was the last time you shopped? Better question is where do you shop?" Lani rolled over on Erin's bed and bounced to her feet.

She marched to the closet and flipped through the clothes. Once in a while she pulled a top or a pair of pants out for closer inspection, but then curled her top lip. The rejected clothes would go flying into the growing heap on the floor.

"You're not making this any easier." Erin hated the queasy feeling. "I should cancel."

Lani ignored her. "Since you don't know what you'll

be doing or where you're going, I suggest you wear pants."

Tables had turned. In certain areas of life, Lani definitely took the lead. Erin wasn't too proud to take the help. What did she know about fashion for dates? She entered the closet since Lani couldn't seem to find anything acceptable.

"You know, sis, you need to come and organize my closet," Lani remarked, standing next to Erin. "Pants, skirts, dresses, short-sleeved blouses, long-sleeved—Wowza! Is your underwear drawer just as organized? You know, spontaneity isn't a bad thing."

"Stop talking and get to work. The clock is ticking. Please, put together an outfit."

"That's hard to do. So much sucks." Lani looked on the floor. "Love the shoes, though. Can I borrow those three?"

"Why do you need three?"

"Don't know what my mood will be when I hit the road. I must say that, unlike your plain-Jane clothes, your hellafied shoes reveal what an undercover freak you are—well, can be." Lani raised her hand for a high five, which Erin pointedly ignored.

Instead, Erin nudged Lani with her shoulder. She did like her heels high. Shoes were her favorite fashion item to add length and show off her toned calves. She did have a tiny vanity streak about her legs.

Lani pointed toward the pants. "Grab those black jeans. They look new."

"Yeah, I don't really wear jeans."

"Whatever. I don't like any of these tops. So, wear mine." Lani pulled off her top and tossed it to Erin.

"I'm not wearing your top. Plus, is it clean?" Erin rubbed the soft fabric between her fingers. It did feel good.

"Silk, baby. Nothing cheap against this skin. Got it out of the cleaners yesterday." She stood in her bra with hands on her hips. "And now I have to wear one of your coarse off-the-rack sale items to go see Juan. Yeah, Todd is on hold. Juan came back. Said he'd separated from his wife."

Erin rolled her eyes. She wasn't in the mood to play counsel for Lani's love life. Not right now, at least. She pulled on the top, which hung loose the way she liked her clothing to fit.

"Love the cleavage," Lani complimented.

"It's cool weather out there. I don't think I should have my girls hanging out."

"You have bodacious ta-tas. Show 'em off." Lani clapped as if Erin had just modeled at New York's Fashion Week. "Okay, time to brush teeth and apply makeup."

"Not that I don't mind brushing my teeth, but my breath is fine."

"He may kiss you. Maybe even go straight for the home run. Bikini wax!" Lani squealed and dived on the bed.

"How old are you?" Erin pretended to be irritated. But the idea that Marc may kiss her added a touch of anticipation that had her licking her lips.

"Let me do the makeup." Lani pulled her over to the vanity counter in the bathroom.

Her sister opened a palette of colors and worked with the intensity of a Renaissance painter. Every time Erin tried to turn and take a peek, her sister grabbed hold of her chin and pinned her in place.

"You don't have time to check the progress." Lani applied blush to Erin's cheeks.

"All of this makeup isn't necessary."

"I'll be the judge of that." Lani continued her artwork, and Erin realized her sister wasn't going to leave until she got a close-up look at Marc. "Now for the lips." Lani bit her own lip as she tried to choose from the three glosses in her hand. "We'll go with a neutral brown."

The doorbell sounded.

"Oh." Erin almost bit down on the lip brush that Lani used to add more lip color. "He's here." Her voice sounded high and squeaky.

"Relax. Stop pulling in your lips. You'll ruin the gloss and have it on your teeth. Good grief, this is not the prom. It's a date and then some hot necking. That's it."

"Not a date," she mumbled.

Erin tried to remember when she'd last gone on a date. Two years ago? No, couldn't be. But whenever it was, it was a freaking long time ago.

Lani looked out into the hallway. "Do you want me to get it before he thinks that you're not home?"

"Yes." Erin rushed after her sister. "No!" She wrung her hands.

"Oh, please, don't tell me you're going to be all fruity and simpering like a throwback from the Victorian period."

"Be quiet. You're not helping. I'll answer the door." Erin took a deep breath. One foot in front of the other and she made her way to the door.

She played with a wide smile, then drew her mouth closed for just a soft smile. Finally she opted not to smile at all. She opened the door.

"Hi," Marc greeted her. "You look gorgeous." He held out a bouquet of flowers. "To brighten your day."

"Please come in." Erin took the flowers. The brightly colored bouquet carried a fragrant mixture of fresh roses, lilies and button poms. Splashes of reds, oranges and pinks made up the big floral gift.

"I'll put them in a vase." Lani swooped in with a cheery smile and took the present. "I'm Lani, her sister, by the way."

"Marc." He shook her hand.

"Ready?" Erin didn't want to linger. First of all, she hadn't really cleaned her house. And then, the longer they stayed there, the more likely they'd be held up. Lani would go into full investigation mode and gladly provide a third-degree interrogation.

"Beautiful place."

Erin waved away the compliment. She could spy a thin layer of dust on the bookshelf.

"You kiddies have a wonderful time. No curfew in place. Don't hurry back." Lani pushed them out the door.

Erin wanted to wring her sister's neck.

She followed Marc to his car, and her phone buzzed. She hoped that it wasn't an emergency that she'd have to attend to.

She read the text from her sister. Nice ass. A keeper. Her nervous giggle erupted.

"Everything okay?" Marc asked.

"Yep. All's well."

Erin texted back to Lani. Yes. No.

She hung back a little to admire the rear view of Marc Newton. No shame in her game as she pretended to adjust her shoe. As Lani would say, "A woman needed something to hang on to." Judging from his profile as he waited for her, she could hang on for dear life.

And there came the heated blush to her face like an alarm bell warning her to stop the fantasy.

As for him being a keeper, she didn't know what that meant. Unfortunately, she was the one who was never kept. Even with bodacious ta-tas, she couldn't keep a man. Maybe if she kept her mouth shut, kept her opinions to herself, couldn't change a flat tire in front of the boys, then she'd have some sort of appeal.

She wasn't stupid enough to think that Marc had any other interest in her than getting his medical release. But then, what did that make her? She was willing to take the crumbs of a pretend date. Gosh, she not only sounded pathetic; she felt low. The alternative didn't hold much excitement, though. She'd be sitting in front of her TV, working into the early hours of the morning.

* * *

Marc exhaled. He'd hoped that his outing with Erin wouldn't be cut short when her phone buzzed. He wanted no interruptions while getting to know her.

He ushered her into the car. His nerves seemed to be getting the better of him as he tripped over his own feet to get to the driver's side.

Her eyes were to blame. She had a way of looking at him, sizing him up, but not in a "damn that's one fine man" way. Instead, he always sensed that he was being analyzed. Maybe his guilty conscience was getting the better of him, coloring his thoughts of what she may be thinking about him.

And yet he wasn't backing down. She intrigued him. A woman who was smart, had an understated sexiness that he found refreshing and didn't need or want anything from him. Would his ego know how to handle her? Heck, would *he* know how to handle her?

He slid into the driver's seat and watched her buckle up. He noted her new hairdo, the makeup, the jewelry set that showed off quality instead of quantity. There was no handling to be done of this woman. If he couldn't get the desire to be around her under control, she'd be the one handling him. He'd rather go down in flames than give up his macho position.

"Hungry?" he asked.

"I ate a late breakfast so I'm not starved. Wasn't sure what you had in mind. I played it safe and had a small meal."

"I understand. Maybe we can take a late lunch, then."

"Sounds good."

Marc drove toward Raleigh, but then veered off to Waverly. Their conversation remained casual, tentative. While he responded to many of her questions, he couldn't help worrying about his plans for this date.

"Did I read that correctly?"

"What?" He knew exactly what had raised the pitch in her voice.

"Did that sign say hot air balloons?"

"Yes." He turned into the parking lot. "Think you're up for it?"

"Oh, my."

Marc reached over and took her hand. "I promise that if you give it a chance, you'll love it."

"What if I freak out in the air?"

"The pilot would bring us down. We'll be in control of the ride." Marc kept his tone even and calm.

"Have you done this before?"

"No," he replied solemnly. "And no, I've never taken a date for a hot air balloon ride."

"Good to know on both counts, I guess. So you aren't qualified to calm me." She looked as if she was on the verge of changing her mind. Marc could see the wheels of her thought process grinding. She practically gnawed her lip.

"I'm sure we'll have fun. I wanted you to experience that rush of adrenaline. A little touch of what I feel about racing."

"I could get that by riding in an all-glass elevator."

He had hoped that she'd appreciate his effort to show

her a bit of what motivated him. The method, however, should have been done with a bit more finesse. He could only claim to be a smooth talker, not a smooth operator. Also, he wanted to impress the living daylights out of her. How many men took their dates for a hot air balloon ride? Bonus points should be awarded to him for originality, if for nothing else.

He heard her sigh. "I can't believe I'm going to do this. I can't believe *you're* doing this. You are the patient, with neck injuries. And I'm the doctor."

"Whoa! I'm not flying the balloon. If anything happens, you can do CPR. Actually a chance for mouth-to-mouth may not be a bad thing." He nudged her arm to ignite her sense of humor.

"I can see you're going to make this therapy process interesting. I must say, you are truly unique."

"So, you'll join me?"

"Do I have a choice?" She looked over to the launch area.

"Always."

"Why don't I believe that?"

"Sounds better than the truth. I would nag the heck out of you until you do what I want."

"Now that's the Marc Newton I knew was in there." She looked at him and grinned. "Let's go."

Marc hurried out of the car in case she changed her mind. Knowing that she was about to share in an adventure that he'd thought about doing bolstered his mood. Walking next to her to meet the staff, he fought the urge to slide his hand into hers and lock fingers.

After the introductions, they headed over to the launch area. As they approached the inflated balloon, he felt Erin's hand slip into his. Her fingers felt cold and her hand had a slight tremor. He squeezed her hand, which fitted neatly into his. When she looked over at him, he shared an encouraging wink. She had no idea how hard he fought to act the perfect gentleman.

This woman, intelligent, sarcastic and confident, reeled him along like a fish caught by live, alluring bait. He was hooked.

He looked up at the clear sky. "The weather is perfect for the ride."

"It's a bit chilly, though." Erin briskly rubbed her arm with her free hand.

"You'll see. Once you get in the air, the burners will provide a comfortable temperature. I did research," he quickly offered when she made a face at his tidbit. "Besides, I'll share my jacket with you and even put my arm around your shoulder."

"How gallant of you. Like a knight, but without all the credentials."

"I hear pure sarcasm."

"I'm an expert and do have all the credentials." She nudged him in his side.

The pilot came up to fill them in on the procedures. "Before we get started, there are forms to fill out. There is also a short orientation. Then we'll be soaring like Mary Poppins. I'm Tony, your pilot, and this is Shelby, your guide. I don't multitask well, hence the guide," the pilot joked. He handed them information to read and the necessary paperwork.

Marc wanted to warn him that joking wasn't going to do him any favors. He wasn't confident that Erin would lift off.

The pilot continued to explain how he used the fan to blow cool air into the balloon. While the balloon lay on the ground, the burners heated the air. Gradually the balloon would rise to an upright position.

As the balloon did just that, rising into the correct position, Marc glanced over at Erin to gauge her excitement level. She stepped closer to him. He read her easy smile to mean that she wasn't going to run back to the car and demand to be taken home. She didn't resist when he followed his instinct and rested his hand on the small of her back. Her body relaxed alongside his. He exhaled with a grateful sigh.

They listened to the rules and advisories. However, for him, staying focused proved to be difficult. The slight breeze didn't help at all. Her hair, fragrant from her shampoo, flew against his chin. Soft and silky immediately came to mind whenever her thick, dark brown hair randomly stroked his face under the influence of the air current.

Finally, the pilot signaled that they would be on their way. Along with the other riders, they used the steps at the side of the basket. With no graceful way to get into the basket, Marc scooped Erin into his arms and lifted her over the side.

"You shouldn't be lifting me. I'm too heavy."

Marc snorted. "Oh, yeah, you're as heavy as a gallon of milk."

"If you pull a muscle, I'm going to…"

"What?" Marc teased. He loved being so close to her mouth.

"I'm going to say that's what you get for being hardheaded."

"Hmm. There's a streak of evil peeking through."

Erin threw her head back and laughed, loud and bold.

Now that maneuver almost undid his restraint. How could he have thought she wasn't his type? Well, she wasn't the type he usually went after, but he was willing to go along with whatever forces brought them together.

"We'll only be up in the air for an hour," Marc explained. The statement was mostly for his benefit. He had an hour to be in close proximity with Erin. Or he had an hour to convince her when their feet touched land that they needed a part two to the day.

"Is that tidbit supposed to comfort me?" She walked the inside perimeter of the basket, looking over the sides. Panic etched across her entire body, stiffening her muscles.

"Either you think of this only as a measly sixty minutes with the sexiest man alive or a thrilling two-thousand-feet experience hovering in the air with the sexiest man alive. If you have a panic attack, you just might have to show some appreciation for my heroic presence."

"Either option includes you. Seems like a breakneck plunge into the danger zone for option A or B."

"I do have danger zone tattooed on my body."

She assessed his fully clothed body. "Liar."

"Maybe. Maybe not."

She opened her mouth to respond and then shook her head. Marc leaned in to whisper in her ear, "Pay attention, we may need to know the emergency procedures."

They watched the pilot complete the various safety checks, duly participating whenever necessary.

Finally they lifted off with a jolt. Once they were several hundred feet in the air, the wind picked up with a surprising gentleness. The basket for the passengers was made of tightly woven wicker strong enough to protect them and still be lightweight and flexible.

Marc shared in Erin's nervousness when he stood near the side walls. The average height was about three feet. According to their guide, the walls were high enough for passengers to feel secure and low enough for young passengers to easily see over the side.

The height didn't conflict with getting a wonderful view. They stood side by side enjoying the unique view of Raleigh and the outlying areas. The sensation of flying over trees, lakes and streams, and a lucky sighting of a herd of deer made the experience unique and inspiring.

The guide explained further how the hot air balloon worked. "Here's your mini–science class, folks. Hot air rises and cold air sinks. So while the supercooled air in your grocer's freezer settles down around the food, the hot air in a hot air balloon pushes up, keeping the balloon floating."

"How are you feeling?" Marc asked, a bit concerned with how quiet Erin had become.

"I'm fine. Guess I got overwhelmed with the beauty of it all. Down there in the heart of things, you get caught up with the small stuff—the weeds. Up here, when you see the big picture, the landscape is so majestic. Makes you realize how small you are in the cosmos." She offered him a small smile. "I sound a bit too philosophical for a Saturday afternoon."

"Notice how warm you feel," the guide interjected. "Although the midday has a slight chill, floating in the hot air balloon has the opposite experience. The burner positioned above our heads with that huge flame heats the air inside the balloon's envelope. It's like having a portable sunlamp."

"Do we have to worry about the weather?" Erin directed her question to the guide.

She responded, "The pilot gets full aviation weather reports from both government and private sources. If you recall, the pilot released small helium balloons to see the wind direction and speed before we lifted off. Up here, layers of wind are going in different directions or moving at different speeds."

Marc felt Erin lean into him. "This ride isn't quite so simple," she said, her voice full of wonder.

"Don't think about the physics. Switch your brain to liberal arts and focus on colors and textures."

Marc did appreciate the pilot's skill in maneuvering the balloon. More than ever, he got a kick out of hearing

Erin's giggle erupt as the balloon soared and floated. Much too soon, though, the ride had to come to an end.

Their guide explained their descent as they watched the pilot allow the air to cool. The balloon then became heavier than air, giving the pilot control of the up-and-down movements using the burner.

Once they touched down and exited the basket, all the patrons gathered near the office trailer. Everyone chatted excitedly about their common experience, sharing memorable moments of their ride. Staff waited with a champagne toast. For several it was their first hot air balloon ride. Marc touched glasses with the other customers and saved the last clink of glass to be shared with Erin.

Her excitement hadn't diminished. She recollected the minutest details. Her eyes sparkled as she bubbled over about the patchwork beauty of the North Carolina land. He couldn't help but laugh when he spied her with several brochures that she said were for her sister, her sister's boyfriends and patients. Everyone, it seemed, who crossed her path during the week would be greeted enthusiastically with tales of the hot air balloon ride.

Her joy touched him. The idea had been a huge gamble, but it had paid off big-time. He tapped his glass with Erin's again and she smiled. Somehow she managed to sip the champagne with the sexiest smile he'd ever seen. The liquid wet her lips, highlighting her mouth with its moistened pucker.

He leaned over and responded. He kissed her with a

madcap intention to simply match her pucker with his puckered lips. Fun and games, that's all.

More science and physics came into effect. The innocent kiss exploded the nerve endings in his mouth. There had to be some law about attraction. Instead of losing sensation, as expected from an explosion of the senses, his mouth acted as a superconductor, sending and receiving sensually erotic messages.

Craving more, he tested the waters again. This time he discarded the pucker for a lock-and-load kiss, sealing her mouth with tender determination. Every time she responded to his attention, he pulled her tighter toward him.

Her parted lips invited him to enter at his own risk. Something basic, more than adrenaline, more primal and uncivilized, zipped through his blood. Its energy pumped through his system like a fast-moving drug that saturated his heart, soul and body.

She pulled away first. Her chest rose and fell as if she'd completed a fifty-minute cardio routine. The cool air now passing between their bodies woke up his senses to semialertness.

"People are looking at us," he mumbled near her mouth.

"They wish that their ride came with these perks." She took her compact out of her purse and checked her face in the mirror. "In our case, that little moment that will never happen again can be chalked up to the effects of the hot air balloon ride, the champagne and the atmosphere. They are all the elements of romance. That's why I know it won't happen again."

"Don't I get a say?"

"Go ahead, if that makes you happy." She pointedly wiped off her mouth and reapplied her lip color.

Marc laughed. He appreciated that she not only saw the humor, but also was affected by the moment. "Here's what I have to say, as the knight without credentials. I wonder because I really don't know if Erin secretly desires to be kissed again. And I wonder because I really don't know when or where the next occurrence will be. But my sadness will reach critical levels if I'm unable to ever touch my lips to those soft miracles of hers. I am a hopeful, humble man who says that next time he will continue the seduction up close and purely personal with his mouth and tongue."

"Tsk. Tsk." Erin tutted her tongue. "You poor, delusional man. My services are with the physical body. You need my colleague in psychiatry who deals with men stuck in teenage fantasies who tried to seduce their doctors and who think they've got it like that." She patted his face, then adjusted her clothes and walked past him to the car.

"Okay, Dr. Killjoy, let's go have lunch." Marc wasn't the praying type, but he certainly did pray for another opportunity with Dr. Wilson.

Chapter 5

Erin couldn't stop glancing at the clock awaiting Marc's arrival. The man invaded her thoughts with the strength of a marauding army taking residence. Once he'd kissed her, a unique bond had spun around her like a web and sealed her in its power. Not that she'd fought hard to avoid the personal contact.

Two days since the hot air balloon ride, the memory of the kiss they'd exchanged remained vivid. She still felt the warmth of his body along the length of hers. The way he'd looked at her fired up the desire between her legs. He'd tasted as good as he looked—a hot, melt-in-the-mouth chocolate treat.

Marc continued to shake up her world. Her internal warning systems had activated to keep her focused. Work had always tended to keep her physical needs at rest. The workload provided no time to think about being alone, feeling lonely. She had her family and her work. With the new project of opening the therapeutic clinic, her personal, more intimate yearnings were tucked out of sight, out of mind.

But Marc Newton, the wonder boy of race car driving, blasted away the covering, breathing life into her soul. Giving him credit for such a rediscovery didn't mean that he should gain access to her heart. He may have certain advantages because of his physical beauty, but he was definitely not the man of her dreams. Too wild. Too impulsive. Too risky. She had to keep that in mind…or be a goner.

"Dr. Wilson, he's here."

Erin thanked her assistant. "Please have Janice join us."

Having her physician assistant at her side served a two-fold purpose—getting Marc on the road to recovery and preventing any mild flirtation that he was bound to toss her way.

"Erin, good to see you." Marc entered the room, instantly dominating it. "You look recovered from Saturday."

She stood up and kept her distance. "That was a pretty cool surprise. But I don't need too many of those. I may not have enough insurance," she joked.

Her six-foot-three, happily married with four children physician assistant entered. "Marc, this is Janice, my PA. She will assist with your therapy and take the lead when I have emergencies."

"Good to meet you." Janice shook hands with Marc. "Here's a gown. Please change and we'll be back shortly."

Erin left the room with Janice. She waited a few minutes, then had Janice check on Marc's progress. With his consent, they entered the room. While Janice adjusted the machines, Erin explained to Marc what they were going to do.

"I want to stimulate the muscles, getting the ligaments and tendons soft and pliable. We'll start gently with heat application along the neckline." She opened the gown and arranged it along his shoulders.

Gently she ran her fingers over the muscles sculpted into hills and valleys along his upper frame. His winces, along with the small knots where the muscles tensed, marked the numerous traumas. In time, they would mend.

His neck, on the other hand, needed more delicate attention. She ran her fingers up his neck into his hairline.

"Ouch. Okay, that's enough!" Marc exclaimed, pulling away from her probing fingers.

"Lie facedown. Place your face into the hole." Janice motioned how Marc needed to position himself on the cushioned table.

"This is like putting your face on a toilet seat," Marc complained. He groaned his way into position.

"Are all race car drivers whiny?" Erin joked.

"Do you know what you're doing?" His voice was muffled.

"Actually, I don't. I learned online and practiced on

Janice. But we'll get you back in the saddle once I re-read that chapter on neck injuries."

"Not funny."

"From my vantage point, I'd disagree." Erin nodded to Janice to begin working on Marc. She opened up his file and jotted notes rather than openly admire his full rear view. "I'll leave you in the capable hands of my PA."

"Will I be all set, then?"

"Follow our instructions. Take it easy—that means rest. And we'll see." Erin refused to commit about Marc's readiness. Having his brain sloshing around after being bruised wasn't an issue to be taken lightly.

Marc cursed.

Erin cleared her throat.

"Sorry."

"I understand your frustration, really I do. Try to be patient." She casually touched his shoulder to reassure him.

Marc grunted his assent.

Erin finished up with the instructions before leaving the room. First thing she needed to do was to complete paperwork on Marc's insurance forms. Her opinion wouldn't stop him from racing. He still had the freedom to move ahead. So far, this team and Marc were listening to her advice, even if they were strong-arming her into giving him a clean bill of health.

No one was going to make her budge on a decision if she felt otherwise.

Not even Marc and his Casanova techniques could

sway her decision. She had to admit he did surprise her by showing up for therapy today. His tendency to be cavalier about it, though, didn't help get her to trust him.

In his world, he must be used to approaching life with a win-or-lose mentality. Therefore, winning was the only option. She supposed that whether he wanted to or not, he didn't have to slow down to consider what the other person wanted. He didn't have to understand life from a different angle. He was prewired to compete and conquer.

Nevertheless, she had to resist being tempted by his passionate kisses. A wide chasm of values divided their worlds. The truth filled her with a certain amount of regret, but also a smidgen of relief. Her neat, orderly world wouldn't have to adjust to Marc's impulsive, frenetic energy.

Once she'd finished up on the administrative details for Marc, she turned her attention to her pet project. She was opening a physical therapy clinic for rheumatoid arthritis and other joint problems, specially aimed to serve the underserved portion of the community.

Funding was crucial. Her success, coupled with her colleagues' help, had started the ball rolling. But she wasn't going to coast and be hard hit when the funds dried up and contributors turned to the next trendy charity.

Private, boutique-style facilities were the rage in upscale neighborhood communities. Donors would have no reservation about supporting their exclusive access to these clinics. However, when the target dealt with the general masses, donations trickled in. The price tag to open and run an extension to her office was hefty.

Funding efforts had begun three years ago. Fruition was close; she could feel it. She wanted the unit and on-going research funds in her mother's name for the fight against rheumatoid arthritis. Once patients experienced the onset of the disease, then coping had to be the next focus in their therapy.

Her practice already worked with many patients, but she also wanted to ensure that people of limited means could get access and enjoy a decent life. Some days she felt as if she'd reached too high for her dreams. Would her research dollars only be a small drop in an enor-mous bucket?

She only had to see her mom's photo on her desk to reinvigorate her purpose. That call to work harder, strive for more, stay ahead of the pack became the rule to live by.

While fundraising receptions and silent auctions generated large sums, the simple, less labor-intensive method worked, too. For the next hour, she picked up the phone and dialed her contacts.

Marc returned to his office feeling much better. His shoulders had loosened. His neck didn't feel tight and pinched. Even his head didn't give the occasional throb at the base of his neck. Day one of therapy he'd count as a success—for his body only.

He had to admit that he'd hoped Erin would be a little warmer toward him. Their date had ended on a pleasant note with lunch and a stroll in the park. He hadn't tried to kiss her again, but they did hold hands and talk. Then he'd returned her home and left, expressing to her that he hoped they could do this again.

Since when did he act with restraint?

He must have been asleep at the wheel and missed the detour. He had started with a mission. He needed the doctor to give her recommendation that he was ready to race.

His strategy relied on his prowess with the ladies. No long-term attachment was on the table for consideration. No more than one date, a few expensive gifts, probably one time jumping her bones if she had a nice body—and she did—had been the plan of attack.

So far, the operation was a zigzag affair that left him confused, switching tactics and doing things for the wrong reasons: doing it because he wanted to or because he wanted her to like him.

He never cared if a woman liked him. Actually, he'd never had to face such a rejection. Well, maybe if he counted back a few days when Dr. Wilson stood in her no-nonsense medical coat and sexy shoes looking unimpressed at him.

"So what do you think?"

Marc looked up at Lionel, who stood by his desk looking expectantly at him. He racked his brain to remember what was his point.

Lionel asked, "Do you want to interview John Lewis about joining the team?"

"Ah. Of course. Have you all met with him?"

"I was waiting to see what you think. I have my res-ervations. So does Steve and a few others. John's reputa-tion comes with that baggage. He's high maintenance."

"But he wins." Marc knew the equation. Wins equaled money. Money meant investing in his com-pany and building a formidable fleet.

Lionel nodded. "That's right. He's got youthful cock-iness that so far has not gotten him red flagged."

Marc couldn't help but respect the young upstart. If the kid didn't control the aggression just a tad, he'd take out a few cars. One driver may walk away and the other may be carried away. Grim reality marked the sport. But that didn't mean that a driver should stack the odds with irrational behavior.

"Schedule lunch with him." Marc felt certain that the kid needed a mentoring hand. He'd feel him out to see if there was any connection between them.

"One more thing…" Lionel hesitated. "We shuffled a few people on the team."

"Because…why? You know I don't like to deal with newbies right before a race," Marc returned, his voice escalating. Lionel rarely made a bad decision, but this one screwed up the vibe. He'd rather the man didn't screw up when it came to his preparation for a race.

"Sam Hadfield was fired. Kept coming to work late. One day he smelled of alcohol."

"What?" This was definitely news to him. Marc had no tolerance for drug or alcohol use in his shop. Not only didn't he care for illegal substances; he didn't need any legal issues to keep him tied up with the courts or with the race car federation.

"He's gone. Didn't leave quietly, though. Spouted a lot of nonsense that we were going to be sorry."

"Sounds like the kid took a wrong turn." Marc sighed. The business side didn't ever seem to stop. Now employee problems came barreling at him from left field. "I think it's a good time for a walk-through. Let the staff see me, front and center. We're too small for people not to be affected when one of their own leaves."

"Good idea, boss."

Marc headed out of the office. He was never afraid to rub elbows with his staff, from the lowest position to his right-hand man, Lionel. He knew their names and their families, and he shared in their celebrations, children's births and, sadly, visited when they were sick or suffered loss. These people from all walks of life were his extended family.

As he walked through the warehouse, his heart swelled with pride at all they had accomplished over the nine-year period. They had signed on to his team, knowing that he didn't have very much of a reputation. But he had a vision. And they had the talent and work ethic that took them to new heights every season. He couldn't ask for much more. Their loyalty meant a great deal to him.

"Tom, good to see you," he greeted the pit chief. Normally he would linger and chat with Tom for over an hour listening to his ideas for the fleet. The man had no formal training, but soaked up real-life skills from the elite in the business. Thirty years of hard, hot work solidified Tom's experience and reputation as one of the best pit chiefs.

Marc continued through the warehouse, letting his staff see him on the floor engaged with their individual subsection of Newton Enterprises. Occasionally he stopped and chatted. In all their time together, he'd never laid off or terminated anyone. Somehow they all got along and did an excellent job.

"Boss?"

"Yes, Martha?"

"The staff picked me to ask a question."

"Shoot."

"It's going to be nine-eleven in another week. I know we've never done anything like this, but we were wondering if we could have a dinner for the military families in the town whose spouses or children are active in Iraq and Afghanistan."

Marc didn't need to think on that for one second. He nodded. Again, he looked out on the floor with pride. "Fantastic idea. What do you need from me?"

"We'll plan it. Of course, if you have any ideas, we'll run with it. But everyone would like to be involved. And then there is the money."

"No problem. Send me a budget. We'll look it over together."

Martha beamed. "Thanks, boss."

After Martha left and started spreading the good news, Lionel stepped up next to Marc. "Nine-eleven is the day after the race. Are you going to feel up to it?"

Marc knew. How could he not know the day that he wanted to race? "I'll be fine. Maybe since a lot of the families will be attending memorials, we should have the dinner after the race."

"Are you sure?"

Marc nodded. His neck and head still protested with the occasional soreness that wasn't intense but carried enough punch to catch his attention. He shrugged off the annoyance and continued meeting his staff. Tomorrow, he'd be at therapy fifteen minutes early to get a gentle workout before therapy began.

Although Marc had met with everyone, the staff had come to the middle of the warehouse where he normally would hold the companywide announcements. He sensed their need for closure on Sam Hadfield's case.

He needed to get them focused and united. "Just wanted to tell you that you're doing a fantastic job. I did manage to get Jerrod Simpson to stop in next week. As you know he was pit chief and then crew chief for the king of race car driving before retiring after forty years. We're lucky to have him share his expertise. He wants to roll up his sleeves and see what you all are doing. Be sure to make him feel welcomed. We're going to close this season strong, thanks to all of your hard work and long hours. Let's not have anything or anyone shift us from our agenda."

Not even Erin "the doc" Wilson.

The second after her name sprang up in his mind, images of her floated haphazardly around his head. He'd better wind up his speech or he risked sounding like his concussion had caused severe impairment.

Why the heck couldn't she stay out of his thoughts? The smallest reminder brought up her name. He was like a kid with his first crush who couldn't concentrate on a darn thing. Problem was that he wasn't a sixteen-year-old with acne.

His irritation rose at being invaded by her. Didn't he have a strong immune system that blocked any obsessive behavior? This behavior was not his style.

Plus she wasn't his type. This time the denial was weak. He frowned, quite perturbed over what was supposed to be a fact. She wasn't supposed to be his type. Obviously, he'd underestimated her. She'd implanted in his consciousness like an invasion of the body snatchers, deepening her hooks to stay in vulnerable places like his heart.

He rubbed his face furiously in an effort to erase any more thoughts of her. He ignored Lionel's worried looks. No one needed to know the turmoil occurring in him.

Finally, he walked past what used to be Sam's locker in the rear of the building. He opened the door and looked into the empty space. Not that he expected to see anything. Yet he felt hollow that one of his staff had to be fired. Plus he didn't realize that the young man had problems.

Already he wanted to give Sam a second chance. Behind closed doors, he'd earned the reputation as a pushover. His supervisors, especially Lionel, got on his case more than once about his soft approach to personnel issues. Maybe he could assist with a detox program.

This business wasn't a multinational corporation where glass ceilings existed between each rung on the corporate ladder. Had he become so far removed while dealing with his medical issues that he'd missed catching Sam before he made his fall?

"You know, boss, he can be easily replaced," Lionel whispered near his ear.

"That's hardly the point." Marc stepped away from the offensive remark.

"You can't manage everyone and focus on racing."

"You've been around me long enough to know that I don't operate well with the word *can't*." Marc restrained himself from having a full-blown argument, not when some of the staff watched them with keen interest. He closed the locker and walked away, wishing that he could as easily escape the feeling of dissatisfaction with himself.

His week only mildly improved with the addition of John Lewis to his team. The young man had enormous potential and a keen mind. Marc saw the familiar signs of an overachiever. He looked forward to harnessing the spunk, developing the energy to be a more powerful and effective instrument. He hoped Lewis liked hard work.

The therapy sessions continued with Erin and her cool, professional detachment. He noticed right away that her routine was to start the therapy and then excuse herself after giving him an update, with Janice, the giant, taking over.

Once he couldn't stop himself and he reached out and grabbed Erin's wrist before she exited the room. He wanted to plead his case for some signs of mercy from her glacier effect. The small embarrassed cough from the PA nudged him to behave. He muttered a half-hearted apology.

By the end of the week, his body had responded well to the intense rehab workouts. The waves of dizziness had diminished. The deeper aches in his back were not as intense, and he figured that, at this point, the muscles needed additional time to heal. But every time he got in the car to do his practice runs, the fire to push his body and conquer any limitations grew stronger to the point of headiness.

Maybe he was an adrenaline junkie who sought the risky and dangerous to fuel that fire. On the track, he looked forward to the zone where he settled low, becoming one with the car as he navigated treacherous speeds. In his personal life, he didn't have a similar state of success. Too many rules. Too many codes of conduct. Too many restrictions that made the simplest act turn into a minefield.

He couldn't walk away. The cowardly streak had never resided in him and never would. One step in front of the other, he'd get to the other side where Erin sat perched in an untouchable fortress.

She'd jokingly called him a knight once. According to her, he lacked the credentials to meet the definition as an elite warrior sworn to uphold values of faith, loyalty, courage and honor.

Well, he'd see about that.

Marc pulled up in front of Erin's office on Friday afternoon. He knew the office closed early, but he'd called ahead to find out if she was in. He doubted that he'd missed her, as he glanced at his watch. The near-empty parking lot was a sign that the staff was heading for the happy hour venues in the downtown area or heading home to relax after a long week.

He waited in his car for what felt like hours. First, he listened to music, then chatted on his phone, then pulled out the dreaded Sudoku booklet he kept in his glove compartment.

If Erin didn't come out soon, he'd probably get tagged as a stalker. His stakeout was proving to be boring and uncomfortable. The temperature had dropped ten degrees as the sun had begun its descent. Halogen streetlamps flickered on, casting a series of spotlights on the almost-empty parking lot.

He looked at his watch again. An hour had passed. Maybe he had missed her departure or she had left early on an emergency. As long as he saw her staff still exiting, he held out hope that she was there. Then he saw Erin's assistant. That had to mean that she would be out next.

Another thirty minutes passed. Now he wanted to go knock on the door. But at this late hour, he didn't want to scare her. His hand rested on the car door handle as he weighed options. Then the entry door to the practice opened and Erin emerged.

Good grief, the woman was a workaholic. He grinned. *What's not to like about that?* he thought.

The wait, though, had made him ravenous. He turned on the interior dome light so she could see him. After opening the window, he leaned out to address her. "You work too hard."

"Marc?" She approached the car. "What are you doing here?" Her smile disappeared, now eclipsed by worry. "Are you okay?"

"I'll be fine when you get in this car."

"Why?"

"I want to see you. Plus I'm starved. You kept me waiting."

She pointed across the lot to a blue convertible. "What about my car?"

"Why don't you follow me?"

"Okay. But you'd better feed me well."

"It'll be a four-course meal."

"Appetizer, dinner, dessert. What's the other course?" Erin counted it out on her fingers.

"Me. Now get in the car before I kidnap you."

She giggled and headed to her car.

Marc could watch her all day long. Dang, she was too fine coming and going. He had no shame with his addiction to Dr. Wilson.

He led her out of the city limits to his home. She had never been to his house, but he was about to change that fact. Like his impulsive approach with the hot air balloon, he kept on the same unpredictable path. It had worked the first time.

On the long, private road to his house, he increased his speed. He looked into his rearview mirror. She followed, staying a respectable distance behind him. It was nothing for him to hit one hundred miles an hour on the mile-long stretch. But he'd be good. He'd keep it at seventy-five.

Finally he arrived and pulled in front of the multicar garage. She pulled in next to him with a squeal of tires. He stepped out of the car and headed to her. She popped out of her car, took him by the collar and kissed him.

No one had surprised him like that since his last birthday celebration when the guys had Dale Earnhardt, Jr., walk into his office with a box of donuts.

Erin's mouth fastened on him, possessing him, taking ownership with the sensual exploration of her tongue. His hands slid up the sides of her slim body. Gosh, he wanted more.

She stepped back, cocked her head to one side and announced, "I'm hungry." On that note, she walked to the door, then paused and turned. "Just letting you know who's really in charge."

Marc's thumb stroked his bottom lip, which still held on to the delicious memory.

He strode past her. "We'll see who's really in charge," he mocked, wiggling an eyebrow. He unlocked the door for her. "Welcome to my humble abode."

"Nothing humble about a home that could house four small families." She walked into the foyer, openly gazing in awe at the soaring angle of the cathedral ceiling. The feature had been photographed for several magazines on upscale homes.

"I figure this is my house until I get old and gray and get shuffled off to a nursing home."

"You want to be a family man?" Doubt colored Erin's question.

"You make it sound like that's an odd thing."

"Nope."

"I do like kids," he stated.

"Okay."

She continued through to the living area. He noticed that the various framed photographs drew her interest. She moved from frame to frame, not commenting.

"That's my dad. You've met him."

"Where does he live?"

"After my mother left, he retired and now lives in an apartment in Raleigh. Says that he doesn't want to be bothered with having to mow lawns and make house repairs."

"Can't blame him. My father is in a senior living apartment. He misses the family and our home, but for the most part, he's comfortable there."

Marc pointed at the single occupant of the next frame. "That's my mother."

"You are a mix of your parents." Her attention was drawn by another set of framed photos. "And these are of you as a kid? How cute you look in that sailor suit, with the hat. Nice." She flashed him a thumbs-up.

He grimaced.

"Wait a minute." She leaned close, picking up a picture frame. "You have a brother."

He nodded. "Had."

She looked at the pictures that charted their age progression. Then there was only him as the solitary model in the photographs. She quietly put the frame down. "Sorry."

"It was a while ago." He forced lightness in his tone. He didn't want to go there.

He walked through and turned on the lights. "So, what would you like? I'm sure my cook left me dinner, even when I told him not to do so. Got to watch the weight." He patted his abs.

"From where I stand, in my nonjudging capacity, your weight is fine."

"Thanks, but I have to fit my body into that car. Every extra ounce affects the handling and that means the speed."

"Don't tell me you're on a baby-food diet."

Marc laughed. "Let me show you my defense against the calories." He took her hand and led her deeper into the house, then into the basement. "Voilà." He flicked on the lights.

"What the—" She turned slowly, her mouth forming a perfect O.

He made a sweeping gesture to the room full of exercise equipment. "I've got everything I need."

"This is like one of those high-priced fitness centers in your house." She poked her head through one of the doors. "And sauna, whirlpool and showers." She headed over to a small kitchenette. "You can make health drinks?"

"Yep. That's my current diet."

"Well, I hope you know that I need food—real food."

"Up we go to the kitchen then." Marc led the way through the quiet house. He didn't keep a staff on the grounds, preferring his privacy. So far no rabid fan or crazed stalker had given him cause to change his habits.

Erin marveled at the room. "This isn't a kitchen. This is an apartment that happens to have a range, refrigerator and dishwasher—all top-of-the-line."

"It's a little over the top. My father hates it. Says he can't find anything." Marc tutted as he opened the fridge and scoped the interior for a quick meal fix. "Of course, his idea of a meal is whipping out bologna and slapping it between two slices of bread with a beer on the side."

"Yuck."

"Exactly. How about steak and potatoes?"

"Since you're not eating, you're going to watch me eat?"

"Basically."

Erin shook her head. "I'll have cereal then. A big fat bowl."

Marc threw the items back into the refrigerator and pulled open his cereal cabinet.

"Oh, my gosh, you really have an assortment of cereals. Even these from my childhood." Erin pushed him aside and pulled out one box, then slid it back before pulling out another. "I could eat this one right out of the box." She looked at the colorful circles that turned the milk into a swirl of rainbow.

"Here is your bowl, spoon and milk. Knock yourself out. By the way, that's all three meal courses in one."

"You must have sucked at math then." She poured her cereal, filling it to the brim. "That fourth one...well, we'll see if your promise carries any weight."

"The offer is still on the table. I am a man of my word."

Erin sat at the dining table watching Marc assemble the various ingredients for his protein shake. Minutes later the blender's motor buzzed as it chopped ice and swirled the concoction into a purple smoothie. She spooned in her cereal, concluding that she got the better deal in the meal options.

"Why are you looking so preoccupied?" Marc asked.

"Trying to figure out why I'm here."

"I invited you, remember?"

"Yeah, but why did I accept? I'm your doctor. Every step of the way, I'm acting like a—"

"Don't say whatever you're about to say. We're adults—consenting and attracted to each other."

"True that." Erin munched on the cereal. No matter how hard she tried, she couldn't answer the question of why she hadn't driven home after she'd gotten into her car at the office.

"So then if I feel the urge to kiss you, it would be okay." He leaned over and softly brushed her lips with his. "And if you wanted to plant one on my cheek, that'd be fine, too." He pointed to his cheek, jutting it out in her direction.

Erin smiled at his prompting. She pushed up from her chair and leaned over to kiss his cheek.

"Thanks. I was hoping that you wouldn't keep me hanging."

"My pleasure." She returned to crunching happily on her cereal.

"Do you want to go home this evening?"

Yes! She had to leave. Even if she'd only lived next door, she had to leave. But after one glance into those dark eyes, she melted into a quiet surrender. "It is pretty dark out there. I might get lost."

Seeing Marc sitting in the sports car had revved her engines. So far nothing had quieted them. She'd be a hypocrite if she didn't admit that she wanted to cry out for more than a peck on the lips.

By the time they'd arrived at the house, she couldn't take the anticipation anymore. She'd tried his cocky approach and kissed him. Dang it, sitting in the proverbial driver's seat felt awesome. Now he wanted to play the gentleman with as little contact as possible. He didn't realize that he walked a tightrope over an alligator pit. One false step on his part and she'd gobble him up.

The visual had her erupting in a fit of giggles.

"Share." Marc prompted with his hand.

She shook her head, finishing off her cereal. "I'm going to have to leave early in the morning."

"No problem."

"No clothes." She raised her hand like a stop sign.

"Before you say anything about getting me out of my clothes, I have to tell you that I do not sleep in the nude."

"Hmm. Some habits should be broken. Although I don't understand the need to sleep clothed, I do have T-shirts and shorts that you can use."

"Good. I don't sleep in the nude in case there is an emergency and I have to run out of the house quickly. Imagine the firemen staring at me."

"I'm trying to imagine it." He banged the table and gripped his stomach as if it hurt. "Gosh, I'm imagining it."

"Be quiet. Show me to my room."

"No problem."

Erin had to admit that Marc had fine taste. Although the place needed the sounds of family to fill the vast open space, the decorations inspired a sense of warmth. Even the furniture didn't overpower each room by color or size.

She took his proffered hand and headed upstairs. Now used to seeing the grandeur of the first floor, not to mention the gym, she eagerly awaited the upstairs decor. The staircase up ahead divided into left and right sides. They aimed to the left and ran up the four steps.

The second floor had a hallway that seemed to go on endlessly with the staircase as the separating point between the two wings. Closed doors prevented any view of the rooms. However, since the doors weren't near each other, she surmised that the rooms were huge.

"Where's your room?" She needed to see how far she'd have to walk if she stepped out for a midnight run.

"On the other side." He looked at her. "I would gladly share my bed with you. Something tells me that would be pushing too hard though. I gave you a room with a great view. It's the one I reserve for my important guests."

"Any guests on the premises or due to arrive?" Erin didn't want to suddenly bump into anyone else who shared the residence.

"No one else."

"No girlfriends with keys?" she pushed, wanting an official statement on the matter.

"None have made it across my threshold. I have a hotel apartment in Raleigh."

"You have drive-by relations with these women?"

"Again, consenting. And in the past."

Erin detected a slight defensive stance. She wasn't aiming to be an irritant, but she wanted to understand what was happening. From her vantage point, she was too busy for anything hot and heavy. Yet, she didn't want to be on his speed dial for when he was in the mood for noncommittal sex. Deciding on what exactly she should expect was proving to be difficult.

"Here's your room." He pushed open the door.

Erin poked her head into the room. She could get lost in there. It was beautiful, posh, like a showroom for high-end shoppers.

"It's just for one night," he whispered to her. "No need to overthink."

She straightened up and turned to Marc. "I'm not

being critical of anything," she struggled to explain. "I'm having my own internal dialogue."

"I know. I've been doing that a lot lately." He reached up to touch her face but shifted direction in midair to play with her hair. "Toiletries are in the bathroom. I'll drop off a T-shirt and shorts."

"Okay."

Erin took his departure as the opportunity to explore her room. Rose, cream and gold accents decorated the room, along with dark furniture. The bed was wide and inviting. She should have no problem sinking in the plush bedding and getting a good night's sleep—that is, as long as she didn't think of Marc sleeping in the nude.

After her quick tour of the room, she headed to the bathroom. The room didn't disappoint. Whoever decorated had continued their good job with the bathroom tiles and matching sink, toilet and tub. The tub was so luxurious, she imagined taking a bath would seem like a deep-sea dive. She couldn't wait to soak.

"Space for two." Marc interrupted her lovefest for the bathroom, having returned to her side.

"I'll keep that in mind. But the first dip is a solo project." Now that she had her sleep gear, she was ready to get the bubbles going.

"I see that I've been replaced."

"Kind of." She kissed him on the mouth and pushed him out of the room. "Come back in an hour."

Chapter 6

Marc left the room. He wasn't crushed that his night of seduction wasn't happening as planned. Just having Erin in his home, a few doors down, made a world of difference to his mood. Now that she was here and they had reached some mutual understanding, he was quite willing to take his time.

Staring at the clock, he felt like a kid at Christmas waiting for the moment when he could open his gifts. She'd said one hour. Sixty minutes. Thirty-six hundred seconds. He sat at the edge of his bed, waiting. His nervous fingers drummed a rhythmic pattern on his knees.

Finally when the long hand of the clock hit the twelve, he popped up. He'd already taken his shower, so nothing further would impede progress. He walked down the hallway to her room, almost whistling.

He knocked on her door.

There was no answer. He knocked again and pushed the door open slightly.

In the center of the bed, Erin was curled into a ball with the pillow tucked in her arms. A gentle snore hovered and disappeared with every breath. He smiled. She looked delicious and smelled wonderful. Instead of hopping into bed and cuddling with her, he pulled the sheet over her shoulder. Her hair fanned over the pillow, making her feminine appeal complete.

He kissed her forehead. "Good night. Dream of me."

Erin stirred sleepily, trying to get away from the sound. No matter how hard she tried to block it, the strange music seeped into her head. Her eyes opened slowly, fluttering away heavy drowsiness. She was in the dark, in a bed. But she knew immediately that it wasn't hers.

Again she heard the music. Sleep continued its retreat while her mind cleared. She turned on the bedside light and emitted a sigh of relief. The odd looming shapes in the strange bedroom had sent her heart racing nervously.

Now that she paid attention to the music, she realized that it was a piano. Was Marc entertaining? Did he have insomnia? Curiosity inspired her need to explore.

She put on the dressing gown and slippers provided for her. What time was it, anyway? She squinted at her watch. Three o'clock!

A dead pianist might be the murderous result for

waking her up. She opened her bedroom door and stood
in the doorway, listening. The hallway was dark: no
lights shone under the various closed doors. No sounds
or signs of anyone moving around on the second floor.
She left her door open so the light could stream into the
hallway and guide her to the staircase.

Downstairs wasn't covered by the inky darkness.
Muted lights were on in the open foyer. She hadn't seen
a piano, but she also hadn't visited every room in the
extensive property. Music continued flowing throughout the house. Erin could recognize the piece only as
something belonging to the classical catalog of music.

Powerfully heavy chords cascaded into trilling
lighter notes. While she was a tad cranky for waking
up in the dark, she couldn't help but be impressed with
the player's commanding touch on the keys.

She turned toward the music, walking past the open
living area, then the library. Another room stood opposite, its closed double doors between her and the pianist. She paused at the doorknob. What if it wasn't
Marc? Only one way to find out. She twisted the knob
and slowly opened the door.

"Holy moly," she exclaimed, marveling over the double shocker of the room's grandeur and Marc seated at
the piano.

The room spanned the entire length of the house with
an open view to the back of the property. On the other
side of the glass wall, she noticed an enclosed patio that
lined the house.

Within the room, she saw in one corner a sparkling

drum set, a couple of electric guitars propped on stands and a standing mic. Looked like Marc had a passion for music.

In the center, on a raised platform, was the grand piano. The bright moonlight bathed the piano in white light as if offering the instrument and its player a stage for their solo performance.

Marc hadn't paused in his playing when she entered. He did offer her a smile of welcome.

What else could this man do? She felt inadequate with only her business as her skill. She couldn't sing, dance, not even juggle fruits. Yoga. She had done yoga three years ago. She doubted being able to twist her limbs into the various contortions would be a celebrated talent.

Marc glanced her way and winked before returning his attention to the keys. His fingers ran across the keys with lightning speed. Erin moved closer, drawn by the whimsical piece that reminded her of fairies frolicking in the woods. Leaning against the piano, she watched him play until the end.

"I couldn't sleep." Marc flexed his long, slender fingers and dropped them onto his legs.

"I heard the music. Had to investigate the mystery of the musically inclined intruder."

Marc raised his right hand. "That's me." He patted the empty space next to him on the bench.

She complied and slid next to him.

"You look good," he said.

"You smell good."

"And on that note…" Marc's fingers rested lightly on the keys, then came to life.

This time the song had a haunting melody that whispered its message. A little sad, a touch of darkness, the notes reminded her of a sad love song, full of lamentation.

Erin swayed into Marc's arm. His serenade gently wrapped her in a soft cocoon, coaxing her into a relaxed lull. She sighed, almost unable to stay upright.

Those strong fingers spoke a language that she responded to with all of her senses. She wanted to cover his hand with hers and allow his hand to take her on its journey up and down the keys.

Instead, she rested her hand on his thigh. His muscle twitched slightly in response to her touch. His muscles grew taut, and she could sense their athletic power.

The mixture of the moonlight, the music and his sexy scent combined into an unyielding energy that drew upon her natural craving to touch and be touched.

Her fingertips ached to be satisfied. She stroked his thigh, enjoying the definition of his muscles twitching and tensing. A slight shift of her hand and she'd moved to his inner thigh, toward his crotch.

Even her breath hitched. She bit her lip. Already she craved his touch, but when he paused on the keys, she shook her head.

"Don't stop," she said in a husky whisper. "It's absolutely beautiful."

"Moonlight Sonata," Marc explained. His voice dipped low and raspy.

Her hand continued its exploration until it covered his crotch. She found it hard, taut, ready. She stroked and coaxed, loving his hardening response.

With her other hand, she pulled the sash from her dressing gown. The panels opened and slid off her shoulders. She shrugged completely out of the unnecessary clothing item.

Nothing should be a barrier between her body and his. She quickly removed her hand from his crotch and pulled her oversize T-shirt over her head.

"I don't have superhero powers, you know. I can't play and think about wanting to jump your bones." He groaned deep in his throat. "I don't think Beethoven had this in mind."

"Yeah, he did. This was a get-your-woman-hot-and-wet song back in the day."

Marc laughed. "Well, if we use your expertise on Beethoven's style, we must follow through on what you just started." He turned to face her and encircled her in his arms. "I don't think this bench can withstand what I'm about to deliver."

"Promises."

"Nor the top of the piano." He motioned with his head.

"Wasn't on my top three places to get down and dirty."

Marc kissed her neck, soft, moist, with a flick of his tongue. Then, taking her by the hand, he led her over to the small settee in front of the fireplace. "I could light a fire."

"Not necessary. I'm sure we can generate our own heat."

"Music to my ears."

"You be the orchestra and I'll be the conductor."

He jumped backward onto the couch with his arms outstretched. His grin looked mischievous and too darn sexy.

"And what's that supposed to be?"

"The tuba section." He motioned down to his private area.

"Impressive. Who brought the raincoat to the party?" She certainly didn't have condoms in her dressing gown pocket. And Marc probably wasn't planning on getting his bones jumped in his music room.

"Give me a quick moment." He exited the room. A few minutes later, he returned a tad out of breath.

"Went for a quick jog?"

"Limbering up. You look like you might cause some damage." He held up the condom packet between his fingers. "Ready. Set. Go."

Erin couldn't pretend to be a sex kitten, at least up to a point. She didn't have a string of lovers. But she couldn't deny that craving and desire to feel Marc under her fingers. She wanted to tantalize and tease.

"Come over here." She'd taken his vacated spot on the couch, seated with legs wide apart, inviting him closer. She'd taken off the shorts and was exposed to his look, his touch.

He responded, sinking down to his knees between her legs. She deliberately didn't help him disrobe, selfishly looking forward to his personal ministrations of her body.

His tongue bathed her with soft kisses, lingering over her breasts with caressing flicks of his tongue on her nipples. Her body reacted as if tiny bursts of fireworks ignited deep within her. She tried not to moan. But she'd have to be dead not to react to Marc's touch. His mouth covered her breast, drawing it in and rewarding her hard nipple with a twirl of his tongue.

His hands cupped her hips, fingers deeply pressed against her flesh, anchoring her as she writhed. Her legs wrapped around his upper torso as her body contracted. His kisses made a straight line down her abdomen.

Her pelvis contracted, pulsing with an increased craving for his attention. He pulled her toward his mouth, introducing himself with his tongue. Kisses mixed with flicks of his tongue set off a chain reaction from her inner folds to the moist center.

She moaned, her head arched back. "I can't hold on." But he only pushed harder against the sensitive nub of her clitoris. Her fingers grabbed at his shirt, twisting it in her fists. She moaned, the sounds guttural, wild, in the moment.

"Let go, baby," he crooned, his words whispered against her moist lips between her legs.

He inserted his fingers with a gentleness that made her want to weep. They slid into the cul-de-sac of her cervix. His fingers curled, beckoning, stroking, enticing the mounting pressure to swell and then to release. Her body felt as if it was convulsing, releasing her natural juices with a ferocity that made her want to wave a flag of surrender. She feared that she wouldn't ever be able to speak after this. But she surrendered, totally, completely, willingly.

Afterward, he eased her gently to the floor onto the rug. She lay on top of him, happy, contented and trying to catch her breath. His strong heartbeat under her ear comforted her with its rhythmic pulse.

"We'll stay here. When the sun is just above the horizon and the room is bathed in the soft light of sunrise, I'm going to make love to you again."

"This time I want you inside me." She shivered with anticipation. In return, Marc pulled her tightly against his chest until she fell asleep.

Marc couldn't sleep. Having Erin in his arms soothed him in a way that he'd not felt in a long time. While he never wanted to talk about his twin or the pain and the guilt he suffered, he now considered the possibility of sharing his deep feelings with Erin.

She moaned in her sleep and snuggled deeper against his body. His arms adjusted before closing around her once more. He hoped that he'd have the chance to get to know her. So far what he knew and saw impressed the heck out of him.

But just like he had his private life and secrets, he wondered what hers would be.

If they did go down the path of normalcy as boyfriend and girlfriend, would his lifestyle be bearable? Already he knew she didn't understand why he raced.

And she'd have to. Racing was too big a part of his life to compromise.

Marc didn't want to be too eager with the what-ifs, even though they crowded his thoughts. Erin had that effect on him. She led him to fantasize. He closed his eyes and allowed his dreams to take form and fly un-inhibited. He sighed.

"Wake up, sleepyhead."

A familiar voice whispered into Marc's ear. He stirred, flexing his feet, ready to turn over and con-tinue sleeping.

"Are you going to stand me up? The sun is rising."

His eyes opened. Immediately he had to narrow them into a squint. The morning light was over the treetops, bathing the entire room in its glow. Looking up at him from his chest was Erin's sleepy grin.

"I made us coffee. Figured you needed a touch of caffeine to get you alert. I'm owed a morning pick-me-up, if I recall."

"And I am a man who honors his commitments."

She slid off him and handed him the mug of hot cof-fee. "Wasn't sure if you took sugar or cream."

"I'll rough it. In a few seconds, it won't matter."

"Keep up bragging and I won't let you finish that coffee."

He took another sip and set the coffee down on the floor. "I suggest you put your mug out of the way, way out of the way. Don't want you to get scalded. I'm liable to have you swinging from the chandelier."

"Oooh, I like the sound of this." Erin stood and did

a parody of warming up, doing knee raises and lunges. "I'd suggest you do the same, old man."

Marc didn't need any further encouragement. He rose up to his knees and pulled Erin down to face him. Her laughter boosted his mood like an energy shot.

His hand entangled through her hair, cupping her head as he zeroed in on his target, those sensual lips. He kissed her gently, stroking her cheek with his fingertips.

She exposed her neck as if it was an offering for his continued exploration. He accepted the invitation with a ready reply of his tongue. It traced the beat of her pulse from neck to earlobe. A soft kiss, a tender nibble, was met by a muted groan, but it wasn't enough. He wanted her mouth, willing and welcoming. He turned her toward him and their lips connected with a whoosh of energy, sealed and aroused for the sensual exercise that was to come.

Touching her, stroking her back down to the curve of her behind, sent shock waves through him. He fought to stay in control, gripping her hips, pulling them against his pelvis. She responded to his ministrations, matching beat for beat, with natural rhythms that sensed his moves before he'd committed them.

In one swipe, he grabbed hold of the hem of her T-shirt and pulled it over her head. Her breasts were deliciously free, inviting him, summoning him to taste their sweetness. His tongue honored each of them, sucking and playing with the nub.

Gently he laid her down. She unzipped his pants and pushed them down past his hips. She lay between his legs. Her hands encircled his shaft, stroking its length to the sensitive tip. His legs tightened, fighting for control.

He wanted in.

But she wasn't done with him.

She reached for the condom and ripped open the packet. One second before rolling on the protection, she kissed his shaft, laying claim to conquered territory.

"You're going to give me a heart attack." He could barely form the words.

"You'd better get to work then." She tilted her hips up, inviting him down the dark lane of pleasure.

He gripped her shoulders. She was real. This wasn't just a fantasy. Being close to her, naked and free, was a dream come true. He hovered over her opening. She was his, for better or for worse. His woman. He slid in slowly, allowing her body to welcome him and invite him farther into her chamber. She swallowed him to his hilt.

Squeezing his hips, he thrust, long and deep. The silent call of carnal pleasure was answered with her hips pulsating under him. Her soft moans mixed with his guttural grunts like a symphony of sensual and sexual chords.

Her fingers scaled his back; her nails raked his skin. Their rhythm subtly shifted from long, leisurely strokes to deeper, faster thrusts. Still, it wasn't enough.

"Harder," she pleaded. Her hands cupped his balls. Her thumb brushed the sensitive skin, adding urgency to her command.

He picked her up and sat her on his hips. They

worked together, the perfect team, grinding and pulsating, pushing fast and hard on their climb to the peak. He kissed her, mainly to keep from shouting with the impending release. He felt her body quiver when it climaxed, and then he finally let go. He felt her heartbeat pulse hard against his own, and he held her on his hips until it returned to normal.

Chapter 7

"Why are you here?" Lani leaned back on the couch with her feet hanging over its arm rest.

"What do you mean?" Erin sat on the floor in her living room with her latest purchase, a houseplant, in front of her. She had the potting materials on discarded newspapers.

"You got your coochie cobwebs dusted and now you're acting as if that's no big deal." Lani flexed and relaxed her feet.

"Marc has a race to concentrate on. I have my work. And at the moment, as you can see, I'm putting this plant into that pot and then placing it near the sliding doors to the balcony." Erin pulled the bag of soil closer to open it.

"I get that. But did you talk about stuff afterward?"

Lani held up her hand with fingers splayed. "It's been five days. What kind of relationship is that?"

"The kind that doesn't need you sniffing all over it." Erin ripped open the bag, spilling the soil on the carpet. She swore, frustrated by her sister's questions, which had not stopped since she crossed her doorway that morning. She tried to stay busy.

"I'll get the vacuum."

Erin waved away her offer. "Don't bother. Just stay on the couch and not talk."

"Okay."

Erin brought out the minivacuum and sucked up the dirt, noting that she'd probably have to use carpet cleaner.

"But I don't understand why you're here. It's his big day."

"I'm not a fan girl. I'm his doctor."

"It's not an either-or. There is a space in between those two people to be a normal, levelheaded girlfriend who supports her boyfriend by cheering him on from the sidelines."

"First, I don't know that he wants everyone to know he has a girlfriend. I'm sure the team doesn't need to know that we are an item when I'm supposed to sign off on his health. And I don't like race car driving. When have you ever seen me look at the sport on TV?"

"When you're dating someone, you do things that you normally don't do because it's not just about you. I think you're so used to being by yourself that you'd prefer to sit in your living room and stick your head in that dirt."

"Thank you—from the expert of using and dissing men." Erin golf clapped.

Her sister's observations stung. She just couldn't understand that being responsible sometimes came with a sacrifice. Avoiding Marc was for his own good. He'd gotten what he wanted—which was for her to sign off for him to race. She'd gotten played by the best of them, despite her intention to keep him at arm's length. And she'd gotten overconfident that a few stolen kisses were harmless. Her body's betrayal didn't help. She'd caved under his touch. Well, more like under his tongue. The memory brought a warm flush to her skin. She picked up the miniature pitchfork to loosen the soil in the pot.

Lani got up and went into the kitchen. She pulled out bread and deli meat. "Want a sandwich?"

"Sure."

Their arguments never got further than tense words and lots of attitude. One of them always backed down or shifted gears to give the other time to breathe. Erin appreciated Lani's sensitivity to the situation.

When she'd left Marc the morning after their love-making, Erin had sidestepped any questions that tried to elicit a commitment from her. She hadn't been sorry for their rousing lovemaking, not in the least. However, in the clear light of the day, clarity had removed any romantic trappings that she may have harbored.

"Babe, don't you want me to cook you breakfast?" Marc had asked her when she'd run to her car.

"Got to get back. This was an impromptu break in my regularly scheduled program," she'd joked weakly.

"Call me?" He'd leaned through the window and kissed her.

She'd kept her mouth sealed tight, shutting out more temptation to another hour in Marc's arms. "Will do."

He'd paused as if about to say something else. Then he'd shaken his head and retreated from the intimate space between her and the steering wheel.

Her hands had gripped the steering wheel. She hadn't wanted to look up into those dark, sexy eyes. Hadn't wanted to throw caution away and open the car door to follow him back into the house. His place, however peaceful and soothing, had not been her reality. She'd known the faster she turned her car around and headed down the mile-long road and merged with the regular people, the better off she'd be.

Lani's voice summoned her out of her thoughts. "Go wash up. The sandwich is on the table."

Erin sighed. Remembering bits and pieces of her time with Marc brought some comfort. Avoiding him, not answering his calls, leaving messages that she'd get back to him left her cold and hollow.

"Thanks for the sandwich," she remarked after washing up.

"No problem. I was afraid that you'd forget to eat." Lani sat down across from her. "Playing in the dirt is not a substitute."

This time Erin didn't pretend that she didn't know

what Lani was referring to. She filled her cheek with a bite of the ham and cheese sandwich.

"Are you able to go see Dad this weekend?" Erin asked her sister.

Lani nodded, scrunching her forehead in thought. "Yeah. Want to double-team him?"

"Sure. He'd like that. I'll make him his favorite chili."

"Oh, make me some, too."

"Sure." This was normal: cooking for her father, making sure her sister was okay, puttering around her house with mundane tasks.

"Next year is the big birthday. He's going to be eighty," Lani stated.

"Every year is a big birthday."

"Yeah, I guess so. Should we plan a party?"

"Definitely. But I think we should do little things, sort of a countdown to the day." Erin suggested a favorite idea.

"He'd love that. He loves getting attention from his girls."

"Just be sure to let him know that his favorite daughter came up with that brilliant idea."

Lani stuck out her tongue at Erin. Competition used to be fierce in their home while they were growing up, especially in the teen years. As adults, their rivalry had diminished into friendly banter.

"So what's next with Marc?" Lani brushed the crumbs off her fingers.

"This isn't the end to an epic. We're both busy with our careers. I have the rehab unit, which is a bigger draw on my attention than I'd planned. Times are hard. Donations are small. Bigger causes are getting the dollars."

"I'm sorry I haven't been more helpful. I kinda figured that you had it under control. Use me. I can roll up my sleeves and get on the phone."

"Honey, I need cash. Or else I'm going to have to put it off. Too many children and the poor need this unit. I've got to work harder."

"Can Marc help?"

"Please." Erin raised her hand in protest. "I'm not going to use our connection to ask for money. Conflict of interest. I've already crossed that minefield."

"I know. I'm pulling at everything that I can think of. Let me talk to my boss. Maybe they will make a contribution."

Erin nodded. She doubted that Lani would be able to get her high-end law firm to cough up a few dollars. But she was also not so cynical to stop her sister's efforts.

"All right, I'm going to head off. Thanks for lunch." Lani looked over at the gardening mess in the living area. "When you stop playing in the dirt, fix it between you and Marc. Don't be like me."

Erin waved her off.

After Lani left, Erin seated herself behind the planter and pulled on gloves to get to work. She didn't have a green thumb, but she wanted to keep her hands busy with a mindless task. However, it seemed as if this project would frustrate her into a minimeltdown. More dirt fell beyond the newspaper barrier. She swore.

* * *

Marc tried not to act like a creepy stalker. He tapped the screen on his phone to end the call. Catching up with Erin was like trying to grab hold of a cloud. If he didn't have a schedule that was filled to bursting, he'd have shown up at her office and demanded time with her.

Of course, he could have gone to her house. But part of him didn't want to scare her away or have her reject him outright. With the nine-eleven military celebration dinner and the race only a day away, he needed to keep his mind clear of emotional clutter.

He had something to prove behind the wheel now that he felt fit. He'd completed therapy, even with Erin's disappearance from the daily routine. Winning was a priority.

"Son, why do you have this big house?"

His father's question intruded on his thoughts. He'd been so preoccupied by trying to reach Erin that he'd forgotten his father was even visiting. "Why does everyone ask that?" Marc asked grumpily.

"Because it's like wearing a shoe bigger than your foot. Makes no darn sense." His father grabbed a beer from the fridge, popped it open and headed to the screened-in porch and to his favorite chair.

"You could live here." Marc noted the increased gray on his father's head. The once-perfect posture now had a slight bow. The lines and wrinkles had set in more deeply.

"I prefer my apartment. This is like living in a hotel." His father took a long swig. "Anyway, I'm here overnight. Plan to see the race and hang out with the guys later."

"They'd like that." His staff loved his father. He was an honorary member of the pit crew. Once in a while he'd manage to get a garage pass for his father to be on the track.

"Heard you got a new sponsor."

"Got another sponsor. Got another driver, too. John Lewis."

His father swiveled in the chair. Astonishment marked his face.

"Here's hoping that it was a good move." Marc raised his smoothie in a mock toast.

"He's a firecracker. But so are you."

"I used to be. Think I'm letting my guard down of late."

"Oh, woman problems?"

"How did you jump to that conclusion?" Mark shook his head. "Not really. The only woman in my life is my business."

"You can pass that B.S. off to your friends, but not me. What's going on?"

"Your mind is a bit too sharp."

"The only things breaking down on my body are my knees. The mind is still sharp." He tapped his temple for emphasis. "Spill. What have I been missing?"

"You've met Dr. Wilson."

"Wonderful lady. She's a smart one."

Marc nodded. His Erin, as he thought of her fondly, was indeed smart, beautiful and funny, and she had a generous spirit. Layer after layer, he saw only per-fection.

"Is she who you're after?" His father chuckled. "Good luck. Like I said, she's smart. Why would she hang out with a vagabond like you?"

His father's joking had the harsh ring of truth with the central question he asked himself repeatedly. "You are the commitment phobe. The one thing that you've managed to stay with, with dogged allegiance, is your race car driving." He shook his head. "You're willing to hurtle yourself around a track at warp speed several times a year. Like playing Russian roulette, if you ask me." His father's countenance grew serious. His keen gaze underscored his words. "Despite my misgivings, though, you have carved out a niche for being a driver worthy of the accolades. You've even struck a bit of fear in your competitors. That's what hard work does."

"Gets harder and harder to stay at the top or close to the pinnacle. Always someone's ready to knock you off. In some cases, these drivers and their teams want to do more than just knock you down a peg or two."

"Guess it's pointless to say be careful." His father reached out and grabbed his hand. "Stay vigilant. When this race is over, you've got some work on the personal front. Go over to that special lady. I do believe that sometimes only one person has the unique key that fits with the soul of another." His father's voice faded away.

Marc knew that his father's thoughts had drifted to his mom during happier times. Their time together as a couple was not always calm, but they had forged a union beyond the bumps with a love that was solid and rewarding. Marc often worried that his father would not be able to cope with retired life alone. The old man proved him wrong, repeatedly.

Thankfully the lengthy periods of depression were lessening. His father was reengaging and seeking company beyond his own. He hoped that one day his father and Erin could get to know each other.

Once family came into the picture, his and Erin's relationship would be deemed to have reached some sort of milestone. But he didn't want to jump the gun.

Heck, right now he couldn't get her to talk to him.

"Is the doctor coming to watch the race?" his father asked. "I'd love to keep her company. We can chat about you and why you're hardheaded." He laughed hard at that joke.

Marc shrugged. He was ninety-nine percent sure that Erin wouldn't come to the race. Honestly, he preferred holding on to those odds. Otherwise, he'd wonder what she was thinking every mile he covered as he raced.

"Well, son, no need to babysit me. Go off and do what you do before your race. I'm heading for the bed to take a nap. I'm like a kindergartner who needs afternoon naps. Makes me more pleasant to be around."

"See you, Dad." Marc did have a routine that he followed prerace. He headed to the basement for a light workout and meditation. At this point, only his inner circle could reach him.

Time to focus.

Time to get his mind in the zone.

* * *

Erin had barely slept. Her thoughts had been split between Marc and the race. Through the night she'd bounced between sleep and wakefulness, wondering if she should go to the race. By the morning, she had talked herself for the third time out of going.

Instead, she remained at home positioned in front of the TV. In a short span of time, she learned in small informational dumps about race car driving, the organization that set the standards and the key iconic players. An assortment of interviews highlighted the facts. One of them mentioned Marc.

The brief spotlight on Marc was a critical report that he may not be physically ready for the race. More importantly, his recent problems on the track were predicted to have a negative effect on his confidence.

The report critiqued Marc's driving season, which had started off with a blaze of wins and landed him in the top three finals. The same report also claimed that he'd choked in the last race and questioned if he had the confidence to be a winner again.

"What do you all know?" she muttered at the TV. She found the unemotional treatment of Marc's season chilling. She hoped he stayed away from the TV today.

She said a quick prayer that he would be safe, win or lose.

The morning of the race didn't help with the anxiety that had sneaked in and settled in the pit of Marc's stomach. He stood in his full bodysuit, gauging whether the sun would emerge to dry the speedway. He put on his gloves and pulled on the helmet.

Nerves never stopped tingling before each race. He'd learned to deal with it. At some point, those mental distractions had to be pushed aside.

He offered his pit chief a thumbs-up.

Marc drove his car to the starting point. He had decent car position considering his points over the season. The engine's roar filled the small car's interior. As a matter of fact, the din of all the engines blocked out any other sounds.

He waited for the race to begin. His hand rested lightly on the gearshift as his eyes zeroed in, waiting for the flag to give him permission to accelerate. He revved the engine and the wheels spun, ready to take off. His eyes followed the pace car, making the lap, until it pulled off the speedway.

The green flag waved. Cars shot out with a squeal of tires.

Adrenaline surged throughout his body like a ride on white-water rapids. All senses were honed for spitfire reaction. He looked down the speedway, strategizing his path—inner track or outer track.

The roar of the engine continued to fill the car with deafening thunder. His entire body vibrated. Number thirty-seven was creeping on his left. He knew the driver's M.O. One quick move and he'd cut Marc off without a second thought.

Marc opened up on the throttle. There was a small space ahead, and he was going for it. He'd already passed the third car in the lead. He wanted that second spot before he went all out for a win.

As quickly as he planned his route, he had to adjust. Car thirty-seven sped up on the inner track, aggressive and not backing down. Marc stayed his ground, refusing to give way. He was not giving up on the opening ahead.

In a split second, the fronts of their cars touched. The impact sounded like two lions roaring, metal entangling with metal. Marc gripped the steering wheel tighter, fighting to control the car, which seemed to have a mind of its own.

The car that clipped his front end flipped upside down, hurtling through the infield as if it had been picked up by a hurricane-force wind.

Too late. His attention snapped back in time to see the outside retaining wall covering the expanse of the windshield.

Marc bore down. The front of his car shredded against the wall, peeling back like an open can of sardines. His head, encased by his helmet, shook and slammed against the car's frame. The seat belt tightened against his body, pinning him in the twisted carnage.

The strong odor of fuel filled the air. Marc blinked, trying to concentrate. Muffled shouts called out his name. He tried to speak, but blood filled his mouth. At impact he'd probably bitten his tongue.

He wanted the helmet off. His lungs cried out for air. The smell of fuel overwhelmed him.

This was not good. Fire had erupted.

He felt the heat despite the suit.

Panic set in, and he couldn't think. His head felt as if someone was ringing a bell nonstop in his ear. He shook his head to get relief, but the helmet held his head captive.

With much effort, he slid up the face of the helmet. Flames scorched his eyes. He screamed, but barely any sound emerged. Finally someone gripped him under his arms and pulled him out of the burning wreckage.

Pain seared through the chaos with an intense presence on the back of his leg upward to his lower back. He felt his eyes tear and his vision grow fuzzy around the edges.

He couldn't take any more. He surrendered to the darkness that swept over him like a heavy dark blanket.

The TV channel showed the live action of Marc's crash. The oversize high-def flat screen didn't hold back on the graphic wreckage of the car's impact. The surround sound speakers captured the roar of the engines, the squealing tires and the announcer's rapid-fire report. His voice escalated with each dire, worse-case scenario unfolding.

Erin slid off the couch to the floor. She sat, gripping the sofa pillow tightly to her chest. Tears welled, clouding her vision. Where her sight failed, her ears heard everything.

The station replayed the accident, slowing down as the reporter described each frame. She didn't care about the details of the other car. She only focused in on Marc and his car. She told herself he'd be all right. Any minute now he'd wave to the cameras.

Without the replay, she could close her eyes and relive the moment leading up to the crash, the crash itself and the aftermath when Marc's car hit the wall and exploded into flying pieces.

After what seemed like ages, the crew and paramedics rushed to the fireball. She wrung her hands as they braved the flames to reach him. The vibrant man she knew now looked vulnerable and fragile as he was laid onto a stretcher.

She had taken to biting her nails, and this sport and Marc's involvement promised to transform her fingers to gnawed nubs. Waiting for information on Marc's status almost killed her. The last scene of him was the paramedics loading him into the ambulance. What was his condition? The announcer was no help as he continued to be stuck on analyzing every angle and then making predictions on each driver's future.

The fire had been extinguished and the cars removed from the track. Marc's charred car was a bleak symbol of things gone so horribly wrong. And yet, the race continued.

Erin didn't care about the race without Marc. She had to get to the hospital. Her thoughts drifted through dark, cold alleys, toying with the bleak outcome.

Through a curtain of constant tears, she tried to figure out what to do next. Get dressed. Then find the keys. Crying wasn't going to make anything better. Her tears didn't seem to know the rules, though. She hoped that she could hold it together to drive to the hospital.

Someone knocked on her front door. She hurried to open it, finding her sister there. A sob erupted from Erin's throat at the wonderful, comforting sight of her little sister.

"I came over when I heard the news." Lani hugged her. "Have you heard anything?"

"No. I didn't call anyone. Figured everyone would be heading to the hospital. I'm going there, as soon as I can get myself together." Erin looked down at her clothes. She did need to change. That was what she'd been about to do when Lani arrived.

"I'll drive."

"Oh, Lani." She hugged her sister again, crying on her shoulder.

"Hey, let's not think bad thoughts. And we certainly can't have you going in there sniffling and red-eyed." She ran to the powder room in the hallway and grabbed a couple tissues.

"Thanks." Erin wiped her nose and pocketed the rest.

"I'll take the keys from you. Get dressed, then let's get out of here."

Erin didn't like feeling vulnerable. Was this what happened when someone crept into her thoughts, her heart? The idea of such a powerful action causing such an unexpected reaction unsettled her. Today wasn't the day to understand her emotions. She only wanted to be with Marc.

She looked over at Lani, who was now concentrating

on driving. Between the traffic lights and speed cameras, their progress couldn't be a flat-out race against time. Every minute apart from Marc hurt. How did her sister manage with her penchant for falling in and out of love? Erin positively felt weak from the effort.

"We may have to park on this side of the hospital." Lani pointed at the camera crews and TV vans that impeded the traffic flow. Police cars had arrived, and more were pulling in. A few officers directed the flow of cars and pedestrians.

"We can enter on this side through the general admission and walk over to the emergency area." Erin could barely sit still as Lani drove through the lot looking for a parking spot.

Finally they found an empty space. Erin barely waited for her sister to pull out the key from the ignition before she popped open her door and stepped out. Cool air hit her face with a refreshing breeze. She inhaled deeply, a fortifying bolster to face the unknown.

Lani accompanied her into the hospital. A long walk through the hospital took her through various departments. Finally she entered through the last doors to the emergency area.

Even without Marc's unexpected appearance and entourage, the emergency area was filled with various people needing care. She craned her neck, scanning the crowd, before she spotted Lionel. She hoped that he would be civil and not be a hard-ass. Now wasn't the time for his irritable, gruff responses. Plus, she didn't have patience with any impediment preventing her from learning of Marc's status or seeing him, if possible.

"I saw what happened." She swallowed the urge to be sick.

Lionel shuffled his feet, his hands jammed in his pocket. "He hit pretty hard. No word yet." The man looked as if he'd aged ten years.

"Was he conscious when they got to him?" Erin asked, holding her breath for the response.

Lionel nodded but kept his gaze averted.

"What aren't you telling me?" Her voice rose. Suddenly her knees trembled as if she would simply crumble without any support. Nausea bubbled in her stomach. She grabbed the man by his arm and shook it. "What aren't you telling me?"

"He kept screaming about his eyes." Lionel pulled her into his arms and held her. She didn't much care for the man, but their common bond in caring about Marc's well-being somewhat healed the divide. She returned the hug.

"Dr. Wilson, so glad you came. I was wondering how to get in touch with you."

Erin pulled herself away from Lionel to greet Wallace. His complexion had a gray cast. His trimmed beard looked as if he'd been rubbing his chin. The tall figure now had a bow at the shoulders. Worry and other stresses had taken residence in his overall demeanor. Who would comfort whom? Lani had comforted her; she now wanted to comfort Wallace.

"I wish that I had been there."

"You were there, in his heart. My son hasn't looked so happy in years."

"You're just saying that. I wasn't very nice to him this week."

"Shhh." Wallace took her over to a seat away from the staff, who had arrived in twos and threes.

"I shouldn't have signed off on the health report." She gave voice to the nagging doubt.

Wallace frowned. "Was he not fit?"

"By all accounts, he was fit. I checked with the other doctors, who were much more enthusiastic than me. But what if some lasting effect of the concussion kicked in?"

"You couldn't ground him indefinitely." He patted her hands. "And we're jumping to conclusions."

Erin nodded. A TV monitor in the waiting area replayed the scene, showing both cars. "How is the other driver? His car did a very nasty flip."

"He walked away." Wallace's mouth thinned with open hostility. "The organization is looking into it. Even with the crazy speed and heavy jostling that goes along with the sport, there are rules. That driver's been flagged before. But I think he's got Marc in his cross-hairs."

"Why couldn't he play professional tennis? A groin pull. A sore big toe. A hip strain. That I can handle," Erin said.

"Because this is in his blood. Even his twin brother wanted to race. God rest his soul." Wallace raised his hand. "They didn't get it from me. But truly this is what Marc wants to do. I suppose if he did play tennis, he'd still be hurtling after the ball as if he had special powers in his limbs."

Erin smiled. The visual of Marc serving a missile-speed serve and following up, if necessary, with a slice backhand was priceless. But he'd survive each match.

Wallace patted her hand. "Good to see you smile."

Erin blew out a breath. "Not much to smile about though."

"Who's the second pretty woman in the room?"

Erin looked up. "Oh, my, this is Lani, my sister." She gave her sister an apologetic smile. "She's my rock."

"Pleasure to meet you," Lani said as she stuck out her hand.

"Once Marc is on the mend, I'm having a small dinner for us. I want to get to know you both." Wallace shook Lani's hand.

"I'm his doctor. His orthopedist." Erin wanted to clarify her position to Marc's father.

"That's nice. Means you're gainfully employed. But I do recognize when a romantic spark has ignited. I'm not that old. So humor me with your company."

"Okay. I'm game," Erin replied. She relaxed a bit more under Wallace's kind regard.

"We'll use Marc's museum."

"Museum?" Lani looked over at Wallace, a confused expression on her face.

"His house." Wallace chuckled. "The place needs people. Wait till you see it."

"Oh, Erin's seen it." Lani batted innocent eyes at

her older sister. "What rooms were those that you managed to see?"

Erin couldn't believe her sister's big mouth. She tried to protest, to lie, to run from the truth. Her face felt as if someone had opened a furnace door. She didn't want to look at Wallace.

"Thank the Lord," Marc's father said with a sigh. "I was beginning to think that I'd have to do the heavy lifting to get you two together."

"No, I think they are managing quite well. Although I would like it to hurry along." Lani looked pleased with her report.

"Me, too." Wallace took Lani by the arm. "Let's get coffee and plan. Oh, Erin, dear, you stay here in case news comes."

Erin stared after the two strolling down the hallway as if this was a normal meet-up. Marc wasn't out of the woods and they wanted to play matchmaker. Well, she hoped they both had enough patience to last into infinity.

"Please let him be okay," she prayed. She would play in any matchmaking game if she could have Marc up and walking out of this hospital. She remained in her seat with her own thoughts as she continued to wring her hands, waiting for any news.

Lani and Wallace came back with coffee and a Danish pastry for her. She had no desire to eat and only picked at the sweet bread after Wallace begged her to eat something. The coffee did help to settle her stomach. She had to remind herself that she was the doctor here. Time to get that stiff upper lip and deal with whatever report the attending physician would deliver.

Finally a doctor emerged. Wallace stood up and followed him back into the E.R. Erin held her sister's hand. She knew that she had a death grip, but her sister didn't protest.

"Could you tell if the doctor smiled when he was talking to Wallace?" Lani asked.

Erin shook her head.

"But did he look as if there was really bad news?"

Erin remained silent. The doctor wouldn't give a clue to anyone who wasn't the next of kin or at least in the family circle. With the staff, media and curious onlookers, he certainly wouldn't divulge Marc's medical status in a public area.

Ten minutes later Wallace emerged. Marc's staff flocked around him. Erin remained where she was but keenly listened. He raised his hand to quiet them.

"Marc is doing fine. Just a few bumps and bruises. They are going to keep him overnight for observation."

A nervous laugh hovered over the crowd.

Lionel waited for Wallace to finish addressing them, and then he stepped up. "I suggest you all head home. There will be lots to do in the coming days. We're not done for the season. We're going to get Marc healthy. Have a new car ready to go for the big race. So we have lots to do."

Slowly the crowd dispersed, exiting in a quieter mode. A few stragglers stayed behind. She wondered if they thought they would learn more or if they needed to be there, just in case. With Wallace's encouragement, finally they left.

Wallace, Lani and Erin sat in the section of the waiting room that was now quiet.

"They have bandages over his eyes."

"What?" Erin had truly believed Wallace's report to the staff. She'd wanted to believe that Marc would walk away from this crash with no injuries. Bumps and bruises she could deal with.

"He's got severe sensitivity to light."

"Can I see him?" Erin felt sure that if she could see Marc for herself, then she would feel better.

"Of course."

Wallace arranged for Erin to go see Marc. But first they had to wait another hour for him to be moved to a room. He'd be under close observation even though his vitals were not in the danger zone.

Erin took on a state of calmness that she was far from feeling. "Are you coming with me?" she asked Wallace when she realized that he wasn't following her.

"I've talked to him. I'm sure both of you need time alone. He's waiting for you, even if he doesn't know it."

Erin nodded and headed to the room. His celebrity status had earned him a huge suite on a floor with heavy security. According to an attending nurse, these special floors came with their own staff and cook. Rooms could comfortably accommodate family members who stayed with the patient.

She knocked softly on the partially opened door.

Her reply was the sound of machines beeping. She

stuck her head in the room. A gulp stuck in her throat, emotion swelling in her chest.

Marc lay quietly in bed, his eyes covered with bandages as Wallace had said. The sheets were pulled so only his hands lay on top with the IV attached to his hand. She approached the bed, unsure of how to announce her presence. Besides, she didn't want to wake him.

"Who's there?"

"It's me." She kissed him on his cheek.

"Erin." Her name was uttered like a whispered sigh.

Her resolve to be the cool Dr. Wilson evaporated in an instant. She carefully got on the edge of the bed.

"I'm here." She took his hand and stroked the long familiar fingers. "I'm here." She leaned forward and kissed him softly on his lips.

"You're wearing your signature scent."

Erin smiled, with a touch of sadness.

"I wish I could see your face."

"You will. Sounds like this is very temporary and more of a precaution. Then you'll sport some expensive sunglasses. Maybe that could be your next sponsor."

"I hope this is only temporary."

"Hey, I know what I'm talking about." Erin didn't want Marc to sink into any depression over this setback.

"Why didn't you come to the race?"

"I…I…"

"Sorry, that kind of popped out." He sighed.

Erin heard the slurred speech. She was sure that he'd

been sedated in order to rest. Obviously her absence was on his mind.

"Rest." She kissed him again, but this time her lips lingered. "So sorry that I wasn't there, my love."

Chapter 8

Every day of the week felt longer than twenty-four hours. Erin had developed a routine of heading to work, visiting Marc at his house and then driving home. By Friday, she was exhausted. That night she didn't make it into her bed; she collapsed on the sofa and promptly fell asleep.

Lani had stepped up to help with the fundraising efforts. Surprisingly, her sister did have a knack for getting dollars from the tightest fists. If Lani kept up with this momentum, her timeline wouldn't have to change. The extra help also afforded her some time to get away to be with Marc.

With his recovery underway, new challenges had popped up between them. The new landscape came with potholes of varying sizes that didn't promise a smooth ride. Of late, she felt stranded, as if he'd moved on without her.

As his doctor, she should be glad for the out. Here was an opportunity to return to normal. She knew the consequences, always had her options in front of her. Yet, she dragged her feet to declare their time together as over. She was sure that Marc was going through a lot physically and emotionally with the post-traumatic stress of such a horrific accident.

Marc had stayed in the hospital for two days before being released for home. The development should have made her happy. She should have been grateful to see him walk up the path to his house, albeit slowly. She shouldn't have hoped for more from him.

But every day in the past two weeks, he seemed to pull further away from her. Now he refused to see anyone, including Lionel. Only his father pushed back, refusing to accept the rejection, and forced himself into his son's life. With Wallace's help, she also had managed to get face time with Marc.

His primary doctor said the dark period wasn't due to anything physical but was a coping mechanism for the mental strain. Erin didn't know how to broach the subject with Marc until he was a little more receptive. Being flipped again in a car had to have an impact, long or short.

After she completed a few tasks in the office, she'd head over to his house. Tension resided in her shoulders at the thought of what she'd have to face today. His mood ranged from disinterest to irritability. Reasoning with him didn't help most times. Other times, she'd walk away until he was ready to be approached.

At noon, she pulled up in front of his house. She knocked on the door, waiting for Wallace.

The door opened. However, instead of the familiar, friendly face of the older Newton, Marc glared down at her, face grim and set, like an unyielding sentry.

Within seconds her mood plummeted. Using every effort, she tried to hide her true feelings and pasted on a wide smile.

"It's not a good time." He didn't step aside.

"Well, I'll see the other Newton, who will definitely see me."

"My father isn't here."

His father's unexpected absence gave her pause. Wallace hadn't said he was leaving, and she had checked with him, just in case. She looked beyond Marc's wide shoulders, but there were no signs of his father in the immediate area. She wouldn't put it past Marc to divert her with a small lie given his current mind-set.

Lately, he guarded his solitude with growing irritation and even hostility to outsiders. His shutting out everything, the good with the bad, worried her. She watched keenly for signs of depression, a common result for someone in his condition. He was a fiercely independent man who had suffered a horrendous accident and physical setback. Usually the subject pushed through, sometimes with a little help from a professional, and with lasting good results. If only he'd accepted help.

She felt as if she was constantly circling him with a

safety net, trying to predict his moods and their consequences. Her efforts received no gratitude. In fact, she walked a fine line, trying to help but not pushing so hard he withheld access.

"Told you, he's not here. Had his own doctor's appointment. Won't be back until this afternoon." Marc turned his gaze toward the partially open door. "I'm not in the mood for visitors. Sorry."

"I'll leave then." Erin didn't budge, noting that no sign of remorse came with his apology. "But first, I want to chat with you."

"I'm tired."

He did look drained. She didn't want to push, but having him slip away to a dark place couldn't happen. Pushing back any doubts about her impulsive strategy, Erin braced herself for his anger while plodding determinedly through his inner sanctum.

She sidestepped him and headed toward the living room. She heard him sigh. Whatever.

Erin beckoned to him. "Have a seat." She selected the single armchair and sat. This would have to be an impromptu psych session. Marc had too many people rooting for him. His father, his staff. The industry wanted his speedy return. She needed him because he had firm hold of her heart.

Exactly when she'd fallen for this stubborn, handsome man, she had no idea. Not that she was an expert in identifying this troublesome condition. Yet she understood the intensity of her feelings for him, how he filled her thoughts in every waking hour and colored her dreams when she slept. His smile had the power of a thousand-watt bulb, brightening and lifting her spirit with its attention. Now when his mood remained dark and dour, she fought against its pull because his pain was her pain.

Having people say "I can only imagine what you're going through" didn't really offer the necessary comfort. But when she thought about how vulnerable he must feel and the stark thoughts that made him second-guess his life, she truly could only imagine the hell.

"I'll stand."

"I'll be quick." She noticed the slight sway as he fought through painkillers and fatigue. "Please, sit… for me."

Marc sat. His face twisted in pain.

"How are you feeling?"

"I'm sick of everyone asking me that question."

"People care about you."

"Got it."

Erin closed her eyes in frustration. "Why the brick wall?"

"Why do you care? Because I'm broken and need you to put me back together?"

"I've always cared. In the beginning, I cared as your doctor. We moved beyond those borders, and I care for you as a friend."

"That's why you turned your back on me. That's why you kept trying to keep me from racing. And you weren't there to see me race."

"I regret that from the bottom of my heart."

"Apology accepted." He cleared his throat. "You may leave now."

"Stop throwing me out of your life." She leaned forward, closing the space between them. "Stop feeling sorry for yourself. You're not done. You're not out of the game."

Marc's mouth tightened into a thin, angry line. His nostrils flared. In an unexpected, swift motion, he pulled off his sunglasses. "I'm certainly not in the game with this." He pointed toward his eyes—red and glassy—before closing them tightly. His teeth gritted as he exhaled in pain.

Erin reached down and retrieved the sunglasses from the floor where he'd dropped them in his rage. She placed them on his eyes. Her fingers lingered on his face. Words of comfort sat at the tip of her tongue. If only he'd let her in.

She grabbed his face between her hands and pulled him toward her. His resistance came fast. He tried to pull away from her hands. Erin wasn't letting go.

To ensure that he didn't move, she kissed him. All she wanted was for him to release the hot anger that seemed to have settled within him. Letting him sink into self-pity wasn't going to happen on her watch.

"Leave!" he practically yelled against her mouth.

"Not until I'm done with you." She forced his mouth open, sliding in her tongue as the ambassador to broker peace between warring factions.

Marc stepped away, holding his hands up as if he didn't want to touch her. Even through the sunglasses she could see his eyes shifted away from her. "You don't want to start something."

"Really? What can you start?" she goaded. "Looks to me as if you plan to stay put in the land of self-pity." Erin kept a close eye on the shifting mood that moved across his face like a passing thunderstorm.

Her therapeutic methods were unorthodox, but everything about Marc didn't fit into a neat box. With a look she dared him to take her on.

"You are just as sexy when you're pissed." Erin admitted the fact with as much sincerity as she could muster.

Marc stepped back and turned away from her. His shoulders had stiffened, as if he waited for her reaction.

No problem, if he wanted to play hardball.

She unbuttoned her blouse, peeled it off and tossed it at his head. The shirt glanced off his head and draped over his shoulder before falling onto the floor. Erin didn't wait to see what he'd do. She continued her onslaught. She unzipped her skirt and slid it off her hips.

"You're missing my striptease for you. If you don't treat me right, you may never see it again." She smiled when his shoulders twitched. But the stubborn man didn't turn.

She kicked the skirt aside. It was time to go hardcore. She unsnapped her bra and wiggled out of the confining garment. Winding it up, she let it fly and almost hooted when her bra landed on his head. Each bra cup sat on top of his head like ears, not quite the version belonging to Mickey Mouse.

Apparently that earned a full turn. Marc now faced her. She could sense his restraint from allowing his gaze to drift down to her breasts. Instead, he pinned her with his death stare. The problem with that move was he'd used it on her enough times that its effect had lost some of its power.

"Just leave…please." He brought up his hands, pressing them together as if in prayer.

"You're almost making me think that you don't like me."

"Erin, I can't be who you want me to be."

"Since I don't know what I want, I'm truly interested in hearing what you think that I want."

"Could you put on your clothes?"

Instead she struck a pose and propped her hands on her lower back. Tenacious was her middle name.

Marc moved quickly toward her. His arm reached around her back, scooping her into him. She didn't resist, allowing her body to mold against his length. With no barriers she could feel every nuance of his action.

From the length of his legs pressing against hers, she felt his quads, strong and powerful. His abs were rock hard against her, while his strong arm on her back practically lifted her off her feet.

She opened her mouth to continue her teasing banter. He took the opportunity to plunge deep with wide sweeps of his tongue. His frustration oozed through the bruising kiss he delivered. She tried to keep up with his powerful thrusts, but the man made her knees weak.

But more than that, she wanted him to touch her

body, to take her where only he could and to extinguish his frustration with mind-blowing sex. She wanted all of it and all of him.

Erin wrapped her arms around him. She wanted to transfer her good thoughts, good wishes, all her healing vibes, into his body. The fact that she couldn't perform that miracle only made her hold on to him more. His hot kisses now landed on the side of her neck. She gladly leaned back for his access.

She unzipped his pants to free his arousal. Her hand slid down between his legs. His sharp inhale was like music to her ears. The thought of him, hot and ready for her, made her wet.

Slowly she took his hand, wetting his fingers in her mouth. He hissed his breath through clenched teeth. *Good.*

Looking directly into his eyes, she kept his gaze while performing the ultimate multitask with his hand. Her hand covered his as it took the straight route to the juncture between her legs.

His fingers answered her promptly, slowly creeping their way to the inner folds. Gently he played with her, stroking, kneading, gliding as if playing a classical piece on her, in her.

The minute his fingers followed the invitation in, Erin knew that she no longer had control. On tiptoe, she tried so hard to keep her complete release from happening. But Marc was unrelenting with his ministrations. Each stroke deep within her marked the countdown toward her release.

As if Marc sensed her readiness, he withdrew his hand from within her. He kissed her, this time with such a level of regret that it washed over her with a coldness that shocked her system awake.

He shook his head. "I'm too angry."

"You're too scared." Erin couldn't help feeling the sting of rejection. He had no idea what he'd done to her upon entering her life. Everything about him had awakened her, made her feel truly alive. Her heart now stood poised on the verge of something new and deliciously decadent.

"I never want to make love to you when I'm angry. You deserve much more. I can't give that to you right now."

Erin felt defeated. Now her nakedness made her uncomfortable. She moved around the room, collecting her clothes. After heading to the small powder room on the first floor, she got dressed.

Tears welled. Although sad, she had to admit to being a little angry. She didn't really have to accept defeat. Anger flared, hot and high, at not being able to make a difference. At this point, she was in hover mode waiting for signs that she could safely land and be close to him—and she couldn't take it anymore. Not today.

She stepped out of the powder room and left.

Marc flexed his hands, trying to relieve the tension. He'd practically thrown Erin out of his house. What was he turning into? He squeezed his eyes shut, replaying the scene. He struggled with his own demons. He lacked the energy to offer her any part of himself.

Did she have to look so hurt? He'd had to stare at her hair to avoid her eyes. He'd had to think about his pain to block her words. So much energy expended to keep her at arm's length. The effort had drained him.

His hand clenched around the bottle of painkillers. Since leaving the hospital, he had more time on his hands than he'd had in a while. Fatigue was a constant companion that nagged and pulled at his concentration.

His thoughts circled in a constant loop around the accident. He'd never forget the impact that had shaken his body to its core. His head had snapped back and forth with a force that felt as if it could rip off his head. Headaches lingered, though they were growing less intense. However, he did need to wear his sunglasses until his eyes healed. Learning to cope with diminished vision through this period had really scared him because it could have meant a conclusive end to his career.

Getting better was all he wanted to do. How long would he be sidelined with injuries? Would further distractions, like Erin, be more harmful to getting his head together for his return to the track? It was a question for which he knew the answer.

His phone rang. Nothing new about that. His phone had been ringing off the hook every day with tenacious callers. He picked up the phone to stop the sound from piercing his eardrum.

"Yes." His tone made sure the caller knew he was being inconvenienced.

"Marc, it's Lionel. Thank goodness you picked up the phone. I need to talk to you ASAP."

"About what?" Marc didn't want to hear any more advice about what he needed to do or how he needed to feel.

"The investigation."

"Investigation?"

"The car federation launched an investigation into your accident. A final report is pending any day. But there are rumors. That's why I wanted to see you. Plus there are general administrative things that I've been handling, and I want to give you an update."

Marc knew that once Lionel had told him about the report, he couldn't bury his head. Maybe his business was the one thing he should rely on. "Come on over."

He struggled to stand now that his leg had stiffened in the low couch. He ran a hand around his chin, which hadn't seen a razor in a few days. Though never considering himself a fashion icon, he had prided himself with having a little fashion sense. If nothing else, he always presented a clean-cut image.

Having made his way to his bathroom to wash up, he felt the fatigue pushing at him, bringing the occasional waves of pain in its wake. He tried to trim the new growth, but after shaving a small portion too far down to the skin, he gave up on the effort. Looking in the mirror, he realized he needed a haircut, too. He wished he could get a barber to come to the house. Sitting in a barbershop would be stress magnified a thousand times, both in sitting in those uncomfortable chairs and stirring up the rampant gossip that would no doubt ensue.

"Marc?" his dad called out.

He stuck his head out of his bedroom. "I'm upstairs in my room."

"Oh, good. I bought a few items at the grocery store. Figured you needed something healthy."

Marc didn't bother responding. His father had been grumbling about his empty cupboards before his injuries. Now that Marc was helpless, his father was taking advantage with an unmasked glee. Unlike Erin who'd followed his request to leave, his father stubbornly remained in his face.

Marc still had to adjust to having someone in the house constantly. His routine was ingrained and he liked not having to answer too many questions.

"Marc, was Erin here?"

Marc didn't respond. He stepped into the shower—a nice long soak under hot water should do wonders for his back. He hadn't done any rehab workouts for several days. At first, he thought Erin had arrived on his doorstep to rip him a new one.

He'd get back on track. Right now, he didn't want to have to deal with anything. The doorbell sounded before he got out of the shower. Well, Lionel would have to wait.

He dried off and slowly dressed. The hot shower had actually felt good. Maybe he could hold off on the painkillers for later. He hated the groggy aftereffect and certainly didn't want to develop any form of dependency.

"Marc, Lionel is here."

"Coming down." Marc was curious to hear Lionel's news. An investigation given the circumstances was customary. But the so-called rumor about the report left him unsettled. Good news didn't require a personal visit.

Each step down the stairs reminded him that he had a massive bruise on his left hip, a sprain in his ankle and a bruised rib. By the time he got to the bottom of the staircase, his limbs trembled.

Lionel rushed forward with arms outstretched. Marc waved him away. No need for the drama. He noticed that Lionel wasn't alone. He'd brought the pit chief. Now Marc was really curious. Even his father hovered in the background.

"What's up?" Marc asked in the middle of the tension.

"Marc," his father interrupted. "The staff." He flicked his eyebrows.

Marc didn't need subtitles to know that his father considered his recent lack of interest for his staff a major faux pas. The reminder tweaked his guilt—a little. "How's everyone doing in the office? I've been a bit out of touch between my fatigue and the meds."

"Oh, no problem, Marc. We understand and are prepared to do anything that you need."

"Despite being sick, I am very much interested in what's happening to them across the board."

"I think we should promote Luis Martinez to supervisor. Then hire one more for Luis's position. Having

John Lewis on board requires more staff. But I don't want to get a lot of people until we are certain that we can sustain the additional staff."

Marc had no objections and remained quiet.

"We have tons of media requesting interviews. You know Martha is going crazy not being able to capitalize on the requests."

"No interviews." Marc shook his head. How many times did he have to say no?

"Hear me out." Lionel looked at Wallace as if his father could help. "I think you should reconsider the reality show angle."

"Why would I need that?"

"Money."

Marc glared at Lionel. The man never changed. Everything had to be motivated by the almighty dollar. All these suggestions were like selling his soul.

"Why don't you speak to the producers? Hear their pitch."

"Do I look as if I'm in the best shape to be talking to anyone?"

"That's the point. They see the human side to you. And then they get to see the animal loose around the racetrack."

Marc leaned back. Now he was the animal. He should take off his sunglasses so that Lionel could see how angry he was. But he didn't want to deal with the pain.

"Lionel, what did the report say?" He was done talking about the ridiculous TV nonsense.

"Rumor says that Peter Williams was paid to clip your car."

"Now that is even more ridiculous than being on TV so people can watch me as if I'm in a zoo." Marc couldn't believe that Lionel was wasting his time. "Is this your idea, Dad?" Marc turned on his father.

His father had taken a seat, listening and fully engaged with the conversation. He shook his head.

"I figured you and Lionel have decided to bombard me with stupid stuff as an excuse to check on me." Marc sounded doubtful.

"That news doesn't sound stupid. If it's true, that's some crazy mess." His dad looked worried.

"Understatement," Lionel muttered.

Marc pushed. "Where did you hear this rumor?"

"Someone in the federation's office."

"And what am I supposed to do with that information?"

"Prepare a statement, just in case."

"If this is true, then this will become a criminal investigation."

Lionel nodded. "I wouldn't be surprised if law enforcement hasn't been notified already."

"Okay, we don't have anything to hide." Marc shrugged off any concern.

"Do you want me to talk to the staff?" Lionel offered.

"No. At least not yet. We shouldn't be affected, other than by the media frenzy." For the first time, Marc felt stirrings to get off the couch and get back to business.

He finished up with Lionel. Although he had been crabby as heck to Lionel, he had to thank him for being tenacious with getting in front of his face with the news. He'd also brought any pressing mail for his review. The pile of mail stayed on the small end table next to his chair.

"That's pretty heavy news."

"If it's true." Marc liked Peter Williams. They weren't buds, but he respected his colleague. No way that Williams would risk everything to deliberately run him off the speedway. Maybe he committed driver error and caused the crash with Peter.

Then what? At least he didn't cause injury to anyone else. The possibility knotted his abs.

His father excused himself to start cooking dinner. "Why don't you join me in the kitchen? We can chat some more."

"Chat?" In the short space of time, Marc was all talked out.

"Okay, I'll talk and you listen."

"Don't bother mentioning Erin." Marc caught his father's expression and sensed immediately that his questions would zero in on their relationship, or lack thereof.

"I ask again, was she here?"

Marc nodded. "Yes."

"And…?" His dad paused for his answer.

"She was a bit of a nuisance."

"What?"

"Tried to use psychobabble. I wasn't in the mood.

Figured that a doctor should listen to her patient. When she didn't, I told her that I'd had enough. Time to go."

"I bet you were more blunt and probably not very nice at all."

"Then if I did such a lousy job, you can play Mr. Fix It."

"Is that you asking for help? Because 'Oh, gee, Dad, could you help me get Erin back' works for me." Without hesitation, he took out his cell phone and invited Erin to dinner.

Marc heard the one-sided telephone call. No need for a wiretap to know the nature of Erin's half. His father acted as if he wasn't in the room, calling him a bonehead. Then he promised Erin double helpings of the dinner he was about to cook.

When his father hung up, Marc bolstered himself for the continued upbraiding by his father. Instead, the old man returned to the kitchen without another word.

Marc followed, limping along, using the wall for support until he rounded the corner into the kitchen. He hoisted himself on a stool, but that wasn't comfortable at all. Quickly he slid off and headed for a dining chair. From that vantage point he watched his father's cooking skills.

Marc tried a softer tack. "When is she due to arrive?"

"In a couple of hours. She wasn't exactly dropping what she was doing to head over to the hostile land."

"How dramatic," Marc remarked in a bored voice.

His father cut up vegetables and scraped them into a mixing bowl. The rice had already been put to boil.

Then he pulled out several pieces of chicken from the refrigerator and quickly diced the meat for the heated frying pan.

"Fried rice?"

His father nodded. Cooking had taken up his thoughts. "Could you at least be the bigger man and apologize to her for being a schmuck?"

"How could I resist such a sweet request," Marc mocked.

His father slid in the vegetables with a touch of chicken stock. The pan sizzled with the additional ingredients. The enticing aroma of the home-cooked meal stirred Marc's hunger pangs. For a minute, Marc was brought back to his childhood. His father would cook those huge Sunday dinners, trying out new recipes he'd seen in the newspaper. His mother would wrap her arm around his waist and look over at her husband. "He's a keeper," she'd say.

Seeing his father in good health, Marc was grateful that he still had him in his life. *Yeah, Mom, he's a keeper.* He pushed aside the sadness of his mother's absence and her new life and returned the memories where his deep pain resided.

"Set the table, please." His father didn't look up from the pan he stirred.

From the looks of things, they would be eating leftovers for several days. Maybe this could have a happy ending for him, after all. Then his father wouldn't have an excuse to stay. And all this matchmaking madness that his father seemed consumed in performing would die a quick death.

"Lani is also coming," his father slipped in the new information.

"Lani?"

"Her sister."

"For goodness' sake, why?"

"Obviously Erin didn't want to come on her own. Can't say that I blame her."

"So it's three against one," Marc muttered. This would be a perfect time to drive until he got every frustrating urge out of his system. But he wasn't cleared to drive. Couldn't argue with that policy this time.

"Do I have to wait until they grace us with their presence before I eat?"

"Yes." His father moved the pan off the range. "Stop acting as if I didn't teach you better. She's not the enemy. Your insecurities are."

"She's not perfect, you know." Marc really wished someone was going to be on his side.

"Perfection is boring. I want you back at work. She can get you there."

Marc kept his caustic reply to himself. But he had no intention of relying on her opinion of whether to race or not.

The doorbell sounded.

"They're here." His father smiled and hurried off to open the door.

Marc stared after the man. He scratched his head as he tried to figure out when his father and Erin had become so close. Despite his sullen mood, he did know how to be a host.

"Hi, Marc, good to see you again." Lani came over and gave him a quick hug.

Her friendly greeting surprised him, and he quickly relaxed around her. She was an energetic young woman who couldn't sit still and didn't seem to like the quiet. Her chatter touched on random topics that carried her opinion about life, politics and rock and roll. Occasionally, he laughed at her comical opinions.

Despite Lani's clear attempts to make sure there was no lull in the conversation, she couldn't make him and Erin talk. Even as they sat around the table, the two merely said grace and sat there with their dinner napkins on their laps.

"Delicious," Lani complimented his father. Then she turned to her sister. "Have you tried a bite yet?"

Erin took the fork and ate slowly. Her eyes closed. Her long brown lashes fanned downward along her eyes. Marc watched her mouth pucker, then chew, before she responded.

"You've got the restaurants beat on this." She took another mouthful. A slow, lazy smile crossed her face. "I may need a to-go box."

"My pleasure." His father beamed.

Marc felt the pointed act of being ignored. Not in his house, darn it. He set down his drink glass with a little force.

Everyone stopped chewing and looked at him. When he had nothing to say, they continued eating. He would swear that he saw the corner of Erin's mouth rise with her trademark, quirky smile.

After dinner, his father and Lani disappeared. His dad made some excuse to show her something around the house. That left Erin at the table. If she got one signal to join the others, she'd have taken off. He was sure of that.

"I want to say something—" Marc started down a road he'd never been on before. He adjusted his sunglasses, anything to keep his hands from revealing how nervous he was. "This morning…"

"This morning I intruded. I wanted to force you to think and say what I wanted."

"You came to help me."

"Yes," Erin answered in a subdued tone, making him feel even more disgusted with himself.

"I wasn't sure that I wanted your help."

Erin looked at him. "What's changed your mind since this morning?"

"My business, my staff, what we've built together is in jeopardy. I need to be there."

"Oh." She looked disappointed.

Marc didn't want to admit that he missed her. That he was fighting a losing battle with himself in his argument that she wasn't good for him.

"And you feel up to doing a full day's work?" she asked after a while.

"I'll push through or else my body will stiffen."

"Do you have someone working with you? I noticed you haven't used my office for therapy."

"Nothing personal. I haven't been going anywhere."

She nodded.

That she didn't scold him left him without a reason to lash out. It also left him sounding like he didn't have any good sense. He rolled his neck, stretching it to one side and then the other.

"Do you mind if I help you there?"

He shook his head.

She stood in front of him and positioned her hands on either side of his temples. Using her thumbs, she gently swept outward. He clenched his teeth to fight against relaxing into her touch and making a fool of himself.

She couldn't simply rub his forehead. Instead, she wore a new scent—soft, sweet with a citrus blend. Her hair was loose, parted in the middle, framing her face. Soft muted shades of color covered her eyelids, and her cheeks were a slight cinnamon brown, highlighting her bone structure. The lips remained understated with an autumn, brownish-red lip color.

All the while, she massaged, working her way down to his jaw, coaxing the joint to relax and open. He wanted to sigh into those soft hands.

"You're so tense. Relax." She spoke as if he'd drifted asleep and she didn't want to wake him.

She slid her hands along his neck, massaging the trapezius muscles. His body responded to the attention with grateful twitches and tremors for her fingers to knead.

While he remained seated, she walked around and promptly worked on his back. She started at his spine and walked her fingers up his vertebrae to the back of his head.

Ever so slowly he leaned his head back against her body until it nestled between her soft breasts. He sighed. Heaven help him. He could barely think.

In one fluid motion he turned and pulled her onto his lap. There she sat across his lap with one arm around his shoulder. They were both poised, ready to spring toward each other, their breaths hot and more than bothered. He kissed her gently at first, until her lips opened with her sigh. Then he kissed her thoroughly, his arms around her, keeping her against his chest.

"Don't mind me. I came to get a glass of water for Wallace." Lani tiptoed around them, retrieved a glass and the water and retreated out of the kitchen.

Marc had paused but never broke contact with Erin's lips. Maybe it was time to stop hiding from his feelings for her.

Chapter 9

Marc's first day at rehab could only be described as hellish. Stiffness and soreness caused his mutinous grunts. But he wouldn't give up. He had to go back today. Since Lionel had told him about the rumors, he'd had a change of heart. The time for feeling sorry for himself was over.

A car horn sounded, and he hurried outside, ready to go. The cool brisk day greeted him with a hearty punch. The cool temperature, blinding brightness of the sun and low humidity added a vivid sheen to the surroundings. It seemed cruel to have a picturesque scene for a day, maybe days, of rehab.

He waved to Erin as he rounded her car and got in.

"Good morning." He stretched from the passenger seat to kiss her.

"You're looking spiffy today." She checked out his outfit.

"Have a couple meetings. Can't look like a bum." He smoothed the front of his shirt. "You know, you don't have to pick me up. I can hire a driver or get one of the guys to take me to rehab."

"It's not a problem. It's one way to get to see you since I'm going to be crazy busy in the next few weeks."

"I appreciate it. My schedule is going to get crazy, too."

She stroked his cheek. "Don't push yourself too hard. You have nothing to prove."

"In this business, yes, I do."

Erin nodded, but he sensed that she didn't buy into his thought process. He didn't expect her to do so. And with their quick makeup, he had no intention of going down a rocky path with her.

Their ride together was pleasant with conversation that could be deemed too sweet. It was as if neither one wanted to offend the other. Marc knew he had the burden of making amends given his behavior toward Erin.

"Are you coming in?" Marc asked. His hand rested on the door handle, ready for his exit to Erin's office.

"Not this time. I have surgery on a knee this morning."

"Ouch." Marc rubbed his knee as if he suffered the same pain. "Here's to a steady hand." He leaned over and kissed her.

"Thanks. Buzz me when you're ready to go home. I arranged with Lani to pick you up if I can't get you."

"Don't worry about it. I'm not sure how long I'll be. I don't want you waiting for me."

Erin made a face. "I see you're going to be difficult."

Marc headed off, ready to start his day with a good workout. At the end of the week, he'd have his eye appointment to check for improvement with his vision. Once he recovered his full vision, the biggest obstacle to driving would have been overcome. Blind optimism was all he had. Its power fueled his desire to return to the driver's seat in all areas of his life. He looked forward to that moment and hoped that Erin would accompany him on the doctor visit.

"You're looking better and better," Janice remarked when she led him into the workout room. "How do you feel?" Erin's physician assistant continued with her usual barrage of questions.

"I'm sleeping better. I've cut down the painkillers. Ready to jump into my car."

Janice nodded after each proclamation. "I believe you. You'll do it."

Marc grabbed hold of those words with a desperate clutch. Two races had slipped through his fingers. In the first he had taken the risk of being aggressive and paid with a concussion. In the second race he may have been a victim of underhanded behavior. Damage to his body could be repaired. Damage to his self-confidence had a tendency to take root and spread like a weed until it choked and killed.

This gnawing threat to his legacy strengthened him

just enough to fight against the traitorous doubts. He planned for a blaze of glory. Do or die.

An hour later, he was done and ready to head off to work. Since Erin's office was only a few miles away, Marc arranged for Lionel to pick him up.

"Hey, boss," Lionel greeted him. "You're moving much better."

"Thanks." Marc got in the car. Sitting in the passenger seat was getting old. Every time he had to get in a car and had to sit on the passenger's side, he wanted to punch something. "Anything new on the investigation?"

"I heard that today an announcement is due."

"Really?" The sudden news of an update caused a knot in his stomach. "We'll be on pins and needles waiting to hear. What's Peter Williams's camp saying? They must have heard the rumors by now."

"They have kept a low profile ever since. I heard that Peter had checked himself into rehab. I think they're trying to minimize the damage. Possibly coming up with an 'emotional distress' excuse."

Marc hadn't thought about what he wanted to happen should the investigation lead to criminal proceedings. The industry was small and, for the most part, self-governing. Considered a maverick by some, Marc would now be the one to cause one of their own to be cast out. There were a few good old boys who would hold a grudge that could have dangerous consequences. He was glad that he had the loyalty of his staff.

Marc entered his office, a bit more somber. Coming in almost every day had had a good impact on the staff, not to mention on himself. Walking through the warehouse invigorated him, even if he didn't have much work to do. Lionel had stepped up in a major way, as had his staff. They collectively implemented the company's vision with hard work, long hours and kick-butt determination.

"Turn on the TV." Lionel burst into his office, followed by a few of his close department heads. He hurried over and punched in the power button on the TV.

Marc barely remembered that he had a TV. He preferred working without a lot of background noise. Now he pushed aside the paperwork in front of him and turned his attention to the small screen. His heartbeat accelerated, pulsating throughout his body, especially in his head.

From his office, he saw his staff heading to the break room where another TV would deliver the news. His attention snapped back to his TV. The president of the federation stepped into place behind the podium. His face grim, taut with anger, set the tone for his remarks.

The announcement was short and straightforward. The investigation had revealed that the circumstances leading to the accident included driver error, with Peter Williams at fault. Additional information, informants and the likelihood of an ongoing investigation led to further revelations of Williams's participation in a gambling ring.

These two news pieces were not necessarily connected. Penalties for the driving error would be assessed. Law enforcement officials would take over the gambling investigation. Meanwhile, the federation promised to launch its own investigation with a vow "not to leave any stone unturned."

"I knew Williams was up to no good." Lionel exhaled noisily. "Now they're going to be looking at the teams to find out who else is involved with this gambling ring. Might turn into a witch hunt. The federation will want to save face. They'll toss a few out like sacrificial lambs."

"You suspect that more drivers will be questioned?"

Lionel shrugged. "I've heard rumblings. There are bigger things than gambling to be worried about."

"Then I must have been in a broom closet. I didn't think people still risked everything to a game of chance and luck. There's no way that stuff like that could be held under wraps."

Lionel nodded. He looked grim, as did the rest of the room.

"So why would anyone do it?" Marc hated the news. Peter Williams—this man who he'd thought of as a colleague—had not only committed a crime, but may have been motivated to do him harm in the process.

When Marc entered the sport, he'd come open-eyed and full of idealistic goals. A few times over the years, the veils were ripped off to reveal a slimy underbelly. Turning a blind eye didn't help the sport. He was guilty of thinking that nonaction was palatable. This treachery, however, was a bit too close to home for him to be apathetic about the sport he loved.

Today he felt sucker punched. People who had shared

time with him, who had talked about families, who had competed with each other but had still held some respect, may not be the type of people he'd thought.

His phone rang. The madness of such a revelation was now going to play out like a macabre production with dysfunctional characters on a stage. He stared at the offending instrument and hit the voice mail button.

"So what do we do?" Martha finally asked, looking to him for direction.

"Nothing." Marc couldn't guarantee that he would be able to deliver a speech without losing his temper. No, the only way he would respond was with action, a decisive win in the upcoming race.

"Need some time alone?" Without waiting for Marc's reply, Lionel started ushering out the few staff members who had camped in the office.

Marc signaled to the last person to close the door on his way out. Then he picked up the phone and dialed. Relief and comfort washed over him when Erin answered.

"Hey, I didn't think that I'd get a hold of you."

"I'm in between patients." Erin paused. "Wait, are you okay?"

"Yeah." He told her the latest news.

"I only heard a small bit. Look, don't let this news mess with your head. That's my professional advice. I have some personal tips, too, to make you feel better."

He groaned, already turned on by her voice. "You're distracting me," he complained. "I want a private consultation with my favorite doctor."

"I bet you say that to all your female doctors."

"Heck no. Cross my heart on that one."

He spent a few more minutes on conversation with Erin before hanging up. Now he had to meet with a potential sponsor who wanted to use his name for a new cologne. He'd never imagined that he could inspire anyone's scent selection. Martha should be happy that he had considered her ludicrous idea.

His father, on the other hand, would find the notion humorous. His once stinky teenage son had morphed into a cologne model. He didn't know which was worse, playing at this image or possibly surrendering to the reality TV drama of his life. Actually he did know the answer, since he'd opted for the cologne. He wondered if they would splice his face onto another body.

He ran his hand over his abs. Dicey.

"How long are you going to hang around all these cars?" Erin teased.

Marc looked up from his desk in his office. "I didn't hear you come in."

"Obviously. I've been standing here for several minutes. What are you working on?"

"I'm writing an article." Marc didn't mind the unusual task.

"You sound amazed by that."

"I am. I hadn't thought about writing anything. But a British magazine wanted my opinion on the industry as the new face of racing."

"Congratulations. Will you be going there?"

"No. All electronic, using email."

"That sucks. I was set to go run home and pack." Erin snapped her fingers dejectedly.

"We can still skip over the pond. Don't need a magazine invite to get us there."

"Don't tempt me."

He gave her an assessing look. "You're looking all wiped out. Why don't you spend the night at my place? I hate having you drive home so late."

"I might take you up on it."

"I'll give you the best back rub." Marc wasn't beyond bribing or begging.

"I might be asleep before you start."

"Rough day?"

"Like you won't believe."

"You've listened to my woes over and over again. Now it's my turn." He shut down the computer and accompanied her to the car. By now everyone in his circle knew that he was seeing the doctor. No one seemed to care, with one exception. Lionel had thrown out his disdain for Erin on more than one occasion. To date, Marc couldn't figure out why.

At Marc's house, Erin showered and put on the loungewear she kept there. She headed downstairs to find Marc making grilled cheese sandwiches. Wallace hadn't come to the house, but had left a message that he was staying at his house tonight.

"This is the perfect meal for these tired bones." She kissed his shoulder, snuggling up behind him.

"Let's go sit in front of the fire. Let me play doctor tonight. Tell me about your day."

Erin carried her plate and a cup of hot chocolate toward the fireplace. She settled among the pillows they had arranged on the floor. The low fire felt good as she reclined and enjoyed the light meal.

"Well, I had that knee surgery this morning. It was ACL issues. The person walked out of my office and will have short rehab. Then I had a case where a child was brought in for a consult. No insurance. No money. Sad case."

"What happened?"

"I saw the child. However, anything I suggest that requires special equipment or therapy will be hard to do for free. My staff isn't working with the expectation of not getting paid." The unfairness irritated her.

"That's tough. What did the child need?"

"She is a young girl with hip displacement, genetic. Surgery will take care of the problem. Given her age, she'd make a quick recovery." Erin propped herself onto her elbow. "This is why I want to create the unit. There are too many people who are in similar positions and need surgery to live without pain. Why shouldn't they? Who wants to needlessly suffer?"

"I agree. I admire your diligence in getting those people help."

"Do you participate in charities?"

He nodded but didn't elaborate.

"I think each citizen should spend some time volunteering. The experience is like a window to the real world. You're working with people from all walks of life, but who have similar vision to help those most in need."

Marc nodded. His hand touched her hair, sliding the loose strands behind her ear. "You're so darn beautiful."

"You're so darn sweet." She smiled at him. "Why don't we pick up on my rant tomorrow?"

He agreed with her. "Let's head upstairs. I'd much rather fall asleep in my bed than this hard floor." He winced as he straightened his legs. "My body would appreciate it, too."

"We sound like an over-the-hill couple."

"I'll cop to that, as long as I get to lie down in my bed, woman."

"Race you up there."

"Now you're just wrong."

Erin climbed into the large bed first. Nothing about this house was small, including its furniture and beds.

Erin watched Marc maneuver his sore body into the bed. Worrying about him seemed to be the constant in their relationship. Yet, she craved being with him, in his company and in his bed.

"I love seeing you in my T-shirts," he said.

"You love seeing Reynolds Home Builders across my chest?"

"Especially across your chest." He traced the company's logo over her breasts. His fingers lingered where her taut nipples poked through, softly flicking his thumb back and forth over the sensitive tips.

"What do I get to do in return?" she practically moaned.

"I did say that I slept in the nude." He pulled off his shirt with one swipe and tossed it onto the floor.

His body tantalized her with its every move. She gazed at the beauty of his muscles, which hypnotically aroused every part of her. Her hands reached out and touched him, wanting in on the delicious treat lying next to her.

"I want you to lie back. Relax. Enjoy the ride." She whispered her commands near his ear, pressing soft kisses along his lobe for good measure.

"I'm all buckled in."

"Really?" She picked up his T-shirt and wrapped it over his hands, inhibiting his touch more than restraining his movements.

She straddled his hips. "Now you're buckled in before liftoff." She leaned over and kissed him.

His mouth eagerly sought hers, ready to play their adult game. No rules applied. Erin dived in, not holding back, kissing him with all her passion.

Their tongues met with an electric shock. She moaned as the contact sent shivers through her. Each sensual stroke coaxed a hot reaction between her legs.

Her hips ground against his, trying to quench a hunger that steadily built to a voracious appetite.

"Top drawer to the left."

Erin barely heard Marc's direction as his mouth pressed against her skin. She leaned over and pulled out a condom, imagining what was to come. The thoughts served to heighten her desire for Marc.

"Think you're up for it?" She trailed her fingers along his leg, enjoying his twitching muscles under her teasing touch.

"Do you have to ask?" His voice sounded tight. His agony was apparent on his tightened facial muscles.

Erin stroked his shaft, paying homage to its power. "I'd say we're both ready." She eased herself onto Marc. Her gasps mixed with his guttural moans. There was no one to hear their primal cries of passion.

Erin didn't need any further encouragement to scream her satisfaction as she gripped Marc between her legs. Each grinding motion invited her moistened entrance to convulse.

While she showered Marc's shoulder with kisses, his hands gripped her back, his fingers pressing into her muscles.

"Hold on," he commanded her.

"I'm holding."

Marc suddenly flipped her onto her back. Her giggle caught in her throat. Her body arched up to meet each plunge, and in mere seconds he took her to amazing heights and she finally exploded. Marc followed her.

Thank goodness for yoga, she thought. She sighed, suddenly drowsy and exhausted in the aftermath.

In the middle of the bed, nestled snugly among the pillows, she curled into Marc's body. He held her in the warmth of his embrace until she sank into sleepy oblivion.

* * *

Having doctors in his life was getting old. A year ago, the dentist was the only doctor he saw regularly, for teeth cleaning. Within the last three months, however, he was spending most of his days between doctors' offices and the E.R. Each visit was more intense and required a longer recovery period.

This time, he had to admit, was an appointment that meant more to him than any other. He kept on the sunglasses even though he was in the ophthalmologist's office. Any one thing that could safeguard his eye's healing process wasn't too much, not when it came to his sight.

"It's going to be okay." Erin rubbed his arm.

She'd agreed to come with him. Guilt swirled in the pit of his stomach for asking her. She was busy, and, every step of the way, she stepped up to be with him. He squeezed her hand, hoping that she understood how much he appreciated her.

"Mr. Newton, come in please." The doctor beckoned for him to step into the office.

"Erin, you're coming with me." He gripped Erin's hand, not really waiting to see if she wanted to come. No way was he going through the appointment alone.

Marc stepped into the darkened room. He had no option but to take off the sunglasses. The good news was that his eyes had stopped reacting harshly to natural light.

Marc sat in the chair as instructed. He patiently

waited for the doctor to read through his file and ask pertinent questions.

"Any fuzziness?"

"No."

The doctor checked each eye, shining the light into his pupils. "You're lucky. No damage had been done to the eye muscle. Retina is fine. Pupils are constricting properly." The doctor pushed back in his chair. "Let's continue with a few more tests. I want to measure your interocular pressure. Don't worry, this is part of the general routine. This latest Applanation Tonometer will give me quick, accurate results."

. Marc nodded. He recognized the instrument and trusted in the doctor's effort to calm him.

"We'll finish up with a retinal imaging scan. I'm being overly cautious, but I'm sure you can appreciate these additional tests."

"Do whatever you have to do. My eyes feel much better, but I need that one hundred percent sign-off that my eyes have healed."

Shortly after the scans were completed, the doctor held up the pictures for both Erin and him. The pictures really meant nothing to Marc. The inner workings of his eyes looked like any picture in a biology book. He'd let the doctor translate the images in layman's terms.

"Well, that's it. Your eyes are healed and healthy." The doctor shook his hand, pumping his arm with his hearty congratulations.

Marc breathed easier. Finally, some good news for a change. This was one item to remove from the list of detractors that had the power to prevent his return to the track.

"See what relaxing and releasing does?" Erin prompted as they left the office.

"Nag. Nag. Nag. Why did I bring you with me?" he said through his smile.

"You can't do without me for one second."

"Won't argue with that." Marc pulled Erin into his arms. He planted a big wet kiss on her lips. "Are you my good luck charm?" he asked when he came up for air.

"Not so long ago, I was the public enemy," she reminded him with a mischievous glint in her eyes.

"You invaded and took over." He pointed to his heart. "Now it's all yours."

"Be careful what you say. I might believe it."

He kissed her again. Her mouth opened as a willing partner in their sensual dance. She tasted sweet, with an addictive element that made him want to continue kissing her.

"What am I going to do with you?" He leaned his forehead against hers. They'd paused in their public display of affection to catch a breath.

"Do you really want me to tell you?" Erin wiggled her eyebrows at him.

She was so confident that he was fine that she raised his spirit when he couldn't do it for himself. She radiated a warm glow over his good news. He only wished that she could be as enthusiastic about when he had to race. For now, he'd take her beautiful smile and sweet embraces.

* * *

Marc looked at the car that had been refurbished. He ran his hand over the chassis as a way of introducing himself to the new model. All the sponsor information turned the car into a busy billboard. But what mattered to him was the car.

His car was as important as any of his limbs. The sunglasses were gone, and his eyes had healed. Bruises had faded. Major joint issues had been diminished. He was ready to race. He was ready to kick butt on the track in the last championship race of the season.

For the next two hours he raced around the practice track. The roar of the car engine sounded like beautiful music that called to him for his best solo. His foot pressure needed to be tweaked as he worked on shifting gears. One of the keys to success was being able to listen to the nuances of the engine, which spoke a language only he could understand.

Marc pushed hard, testing his focus and stamina. His first practice run stoked the desire to race. The unsettled feeling he'd nursed since his accident dissipated. Now he looked forward to next week when he could push the gas to the floor and head down the speedway.

By the time he'd emerged from the car, his spirits soared as if at a revival. He and his pit crew high-fived. They knew how important getting behind the wheel was to him. Everyone from the office building attended, cheering him on lap after lap.

"There's a pull to the right. But overall, this is an awesome job."

"I thought so. We can adjust the rear spring coil," his crew chief replied.

Marc spent the remainder of the day in revved mode. The car's handling of the track had stoked his enthusiasm. Anyone outside the industry and who wasn't an enthusiast couldn't understand the compelling need for this level of speed and the physical rigors of the sport. But he loved every minute of it.

Erin stepped into her dress and let it fall to her ankles. Not too often did she get to play dress-up. The occasion this time was superclose to her heart. She'd wear a potato sack if that was the only item available.

The dedication of the rehab unit would bring out the local politicians, her esteemed colleagues and community activists. For her purposes, the celebrity crowd was only important for coverage. Otherwise, nothing had changed about her mission. She wanted to serve those with limited to no income.

Her dream had come true.

"Are you ready?" Lani entered the room. "You look stunning, big sis."

"You do, too. Didn't think I'd like the emerald-green in that style, but you are rocking it."

"I know, right?" Lani swirled in big circles. "You in that midnight-blue with your back out are sexy and pretty all at the same time."

Erin wiggled her shoulders. She might get pneumonia with her back exposed in the fall weather, but it was worth it. Not to mention, she was about to add to the fashion discomfort with four-inch heels.

"Oooh, I must borrow those," Lani said when she saw the shoes.

"Good luck with that thought."

"I'm not worried. You'll need my help, and you'll have to make an exchange with the shoes. Remember that's how I got the red spiked heels, along with the black sandals with the right amount of bling on the straps."

Erin and Lani took a limo, an added touch that she was happy to splurge for. When they arrived at the party, she allowed Lani to go in front of her. She'd let the cameras capture her beauty, and maybe she could escape with only a few words. Lani strutted as if she was the woman in charge.

Her plan worked. The local media swarmed Lani, who was only too happy to play spokeswoman. Her natural exuberance enticed the interviewers, and she got out all the important facts about the new rehab.

Erin couldn't escape the photo ops with her guests though. She managed it all with grace. These were the people who had donated, many times for some, when she'd come knocking. They had no idea how much this meant to her and her family. Today the facility had become a reality and would carry the name of her mother.

"You look good enough to…" Marc's familiar voice lowered. His mouth brushed her ear. "Good enough to kiss, lick, eat."

She blushed with a grin from ear to ear. Her body

responded to his voice from the first word, and then his sexy declaration warmed her body. A photographer snapped their picture as she turned her head toward his mouth.

"This is fantastic. All your hard work paid off."

"What about my hard work? I carried the load, too." Lani placed her arms around both of them.

Erin turned to her. "Yes, you were like a little Hercules for me in the homestretch. You did good, little sis."

"It did help when Marc wrote us a check."

"What? Why didn't you tell me?" Erin addressed the question to both of them.

"I'm not sure why it came out now." Marc pointedly looked at Lani, who chose to ignore his nonverbal cues.

"You didn't have to do that." Erin wanted to add that she'd rather he didn't. At this late date, she still tried to keep a line between work and play on certain matters. "I don't want you to feel pressured to contribute to my causes just because…" He hadn't really shared if he believed in volunteering and donating. The mind-set mattered to her, which was why she didn't want him to simply throw money at her.

"I can practically hear the wheels grinding in your brain." He pulled two glasses of champagne off a passing waiter's tray and handed one to Erin.

Erin raised her champagne glass. Marc followed. They didn't say much, but did toast to the well-being of the unit.

Marc walked through the warehouse. None of his employees were at their stations. The place was eerily quiet. It was Thursday with a race on the weekend. Why wasn't the place hopping with activity?

"Hello?" His voice echoed. What the heck was going on?

He walked toward his office. Were they going to prank him? Now wasn't the time for shenanigans. "Yo, guys, where are you?"

"Mr. Newton, I'm the sheriff."

"Yes?" Marc didn't have to ask if everything was okay. One look at the stern, hardened countenance of the man who stood in his office said it all. He extended a sheaf of papers—very official documents with seal imprints and signatures. Seeing his staff standing to the side in a huddle spoke volumes, except why they were in his office.

"We have a search warrant for Lionel's computer." The sheriff handed him the paperwork.

Marc skimmed it, still recovering from the shock that the law was in there looking at Lionel's desk. Where was Lionel?

"Your guy has been arrested," the sheriff remarked, as if reading his mind.

"For?"

"Gambling."

Marc felt his knees go weak. They had to be wrong. Of all the people, Lionel was his right hand. Marc shook his head to clear away the confusion. Lionel had been upset when they had learned that Peter Williams had deliberately clipped his car.

Well, come to think of it, he had *thought* that Lionel was upset.

"We're also looking for John Lewis."

All the dire warnings about Lewis came to mind. Betrayal upon betrayal stacked against him. From the most senior employee to one of the most recent hires, Marc felt used. His staff was used.

Marc finished up with the police. Lewis wasn't onsite. Lionel was in custody. Now what?

His world seemed torn beyond repair. Years of investment of time and trust. He'd blindly believed everything Lionel said and did. He'd even trusted him with his deepest fears.

The media swooped down before the police pulled away. Before, they had shown concern about his well-being, but now they treated him with suspicion. How could he not know what his top employee was up to?

"Son, I heard. First thing, get a lawyer." His father stood in his office, looking indignant. "I'm glad they nabbed him at his house. It's bad enough that they're searching this facility, but no one needed to see him get arrested on the premises."

"The problem is that I don't know who else on my staff is guilty of the same thing. This is like a tumor with far-reaching destructive power."

"I'm sure they're worried for a variety of reasons. And what's this I hear about the Lewis guy? He's dirty, too?"

Marc switched on the TV, knowing that he may cringe.

"It's the number-one news story for the noon hour."

Marc and his father listened to the brief update on Lionel's arrest. Footage showed Lionel being taken from his home in the early morning, his head bowed and turned from the cameras as he was led out. Additional footage showed the police taking Lionel's computer and paperwork from his office building. Then the story closed with the reporter mentioning that an unnamed source was helping with the investigation.

"Well, that's that," his father said as he turned off the TV.

Marc shook his head. "I wish that it was so simple."

In the lower level of Marc's house Erin sat on the weight bench watching him work out into the second hour. His brutal intensity had shot through the roof after Lionel's arrest and only gotten worse after his admission of guilt. She suspected that somewhere deep inside, Marc had hoped that it was a big mistake. His former manager also denied Marc's involvement. The small gesture helped somewhat, but still left pundits divided over Marc's complete innocence. His reputation was taking a hammering.

As if that wasn't enough, they'd learned that John Lewis was the unnamed source who had identified all the gamblers. In return he received a lighter sentence at a minimum-security facility for his own involvement in the gambling ring. All this publicity before the race amounted to a lot of pressure that Marc bravely aimed to shoulder. Erin worried that he could crack under the weight.

Once more, she tried to reason with him. "Marc, seriously, why can't you skip this race? I'm concerned. I'm not going to lie."

He jogged on the treadmill. Sweat poured off his body. She didn't doubt that he could get into shape. But he was cramming the training into a couple days. She was concerned that his energy drinks weren't enough calories for the workouts.

He didn't respond. But she didn't repeat her question. She knew he heard her. Finally the machine beeped the end to its cycle. He stepped off, breathing heavily. She handed him a bottle of water to hydrate.

"Thanks." He drank the entire bottle. "You're not going to talk me out of this, Erin. I'm going to do this."

He grabbed his towel and headed for the recumbent bike.

"Will you at least eat?"

"I'll eat."

"I'll fix you a meal. Are you almost done?"

He nodded. She could tell he'd already dismissed her.

Erin headed upstairs to the kitchen. She'd never been around a professional athlete to know what their mental state was before an event. She supposed Marc had his routine. He probably also retreated into his head to prepare.

She simply wanted to make sure that head wasn't still injured. Although he'd been cleared, she was wary. Flying around a track and experiencing dizziness or blurred vision could have catastrophic consequences. For her to be sure, she'd need him to be honest about his recovery.

His dogged intent to participate and win meant that he would will himself through any obstacles, including his health. She sighed.

By the time he'd finished working out and showered, she had a meal of grilled salmon and fresh vegetables ready for him.

"I know you're worried." He cut into the salmon. "I'm not. When you're about to go into surgery, you're in a zone."

"Yes. I prepare and get myself mentally ready." She set down her fork. "However, I'm not risking my life."

"You don't get it."

"I'm trying."

He shook his head. "No. You don't understand because it doesn't fit into your low-risk world."

"This isn't about you racing. I'm only worried about this particular race."

"Would you have cleared me if you had the absolute power to do so?"

She didn't respond.

"You'd ground me because of your fears," he accused.

"I give my medical opinions for other athletes and people with dangerous jobs. I assess and make my evaluation. Not once have I had to regret my decision."

"So maybe it's a control thing. You are no longer able to overthink my situation and now it's killing you."

"My opinion means so little to you?"

"I'm learning to listen to my gut. I've been listening to people all around me. That hasn't done me any favors. Everyone wants a piece of me. They're sure as heck serving me up right now." He pushed away his plate. "What do you want from me?"

Erin sat back, stunned by Marc's cold attack.

He waved off any chance for her to reply. "I know. You want peace of mind...for you."

His frosty approach crept through her, chilling every part to match the temperature in his cold, angry gaze.

"I can see in your eyes the way you think. No matter what you say I know that my job will always come between us."

"I've never asked you to quit."

"Asking me to take it slow or to take it easy is just as bad."

"Showing I care is a crime?" She pushed back. "I didn't realize loving you was going to hurt so bad."

He paused. With a shake of his head, as if wiping away a thought, he charged, "Don't try to cage me with your feelings."

Erin stared down at the salmon. She'd lost her appetite. She'd lost much more than that in the past five minutes.

"What I feel for you was never intended to be in exchange for your life's passion. And yet, what you do does scare me like nothing else in my life."

"I know."

Erin waited, but he said nothing further. She wanted to tell him that they could work on this together. But there was finality in his words that told her he wasn't going to compromise.

The weeks between the races, they were an ideal couple, loving and caring for each other. Maybe he was right. She couldn't handle what he did for a living.

Sadness seeped its way into her heart, filling it with a sense of loss. She didn't need the official memo that Marc was ending the relationship. She offered nothing at a time that he needed her support. Just loving him wasn't enough.

She left shortly afterward, wishing him well.

Chapter 10

Marc had to give his staff full credit for organizing the nine-eleven military personnel and family celebration. The event had to be postponed due to the injuries he'd sustained in the last race. He'd tried to have the staff continue since everything had been planned and paid for. However, the community, the military families and staff agreed to postpone for his sake. He appreciated the chance to celebrate with them at his full capacity. Even the community business leaders had stepped up to provide many of the necessary items and children's activities free of charge.

The fraternal lodge centered in the middle of the city hosted the event. Moon bounces, puppet stages and other portable outdoor toys took over the parking lot. The city had closed several cross streets to provide for overflow parking. The military families and the community planned to unite for the celebration. Marc felt a sense of pride that the city council and mayor had shown such support.

"Son, they love you in this place." His father stood next to him. Marc was certain there was the gleam of an unshed tear in his father's eye. "I told them that you were my son."

"Uh-oh."

"I got a free funnel cake and a phone number."

"Go on with your bad self."

"In all seriousness, Marc, I'm very proud of you."

He hugged his dad. Sometimes words weren't enough to convey how much he loved his father. They were a team united beyond father and son. Life had dealt them some bad blows, with an untimely death and a divorce that had ripped apart the family. But together, they'd overcome so much. He dearly loved the old man. As he looked out over the faces of the military families, he hoped that they had a supportive network for the trying times they'd gone through and those yet to come.

"I say we go mingle and make some people smile today." His father led the way, snaking through the numerous tables to meet the families.

Marc shook hands, took photos with kids, spouses. He introduced families to each other, hoping that they would continue contact after the festivities were a memory. The innocent laughter of the children particularly struck him. Looking at them made him ache for the time when he would have his own family.

His family. He'd never dwelled on the idea. He'd been in such constant mourning over his brother that he hadn't ever wanted to think about caring and worrying over a child of his own. Until now. Before he could deliberate on this frightening, but exciting, revelation, his attention was pulled away by the party organizer.

He'd volunteered to serve the dinner. He and several of his staff ran the plates to the tables. In his estimation, there had to be about seventy families that attended. Lots of work kept him busy. He knew at the end of the day that he'd be lying on the couch—exhausted and alone.

"Need help?"

Marc looked up from spooning macaroni and cheese onto a plate. He felt a bit flustered seeing Erin present. He filled up the plate and handed it to her.

"I figured you'd need help. I wanted to be here with these families." She didn't look at him when she spoke. "I won't stay long."

"You can if you want to."

She didn't respond.

Marc spooned out the food while she carried it to the tables. Neither one spoke to each other, only if necessary. Even his father's light banter couldn't perform a miracle and fix what was clearly broken.

After he ate, Marc stayed on one side of the room. He could keep an eye on Erin and switch sides with her if she had to come his way. After talking to a family with a newborn baby, he shifted his vantage point to seek her out. No sign of her. He searched every inch of the lodge and then headed outside.

She had her pocketbook over her shoulder. Her apparent departure had been stopped by a young man who was clearly interested in her. He stood close, and she had her hand on the man's forearm. He watched, waiting for her to remove it. Really, there was no need to touch the stranger.

Was the guy writing his phone number?

Marc inched forward. He couldn't step out into the open without being seen. And for all intents and purposes, he didn't care what Erin did.

Then they hugged. He couldn't determine if it was a casual hug or an "oh, you smell good and feel good, I want to hug you some more" kind of hug. If pressed, he'd have to go with the second option.

He tried to act as if none of the drama mattered. He told himself he was glad she was leaving. He turned to head back to the celebration.

"For a minute, I thought you'd have gone over there and challenged the guy to a duel."

"You're not funny, Dad." Marc walked past him, irritated by his chuckle and irritated at being caught watching.

By the end of the evening, his mood had considerably lightened. The event was a smashing success. Many of the families publicly shared their appreciation for the city and his staff. He was only too happy to praise them, too, for a job well done.

* * *

Marc awoke the next day, groggy and heavyhearted. One of his rituals was to go visit the hospital for sick children before his races, an activity inspired by his brother's short life. He headed off, looking forward to seeing the new and not-so-new faces.

Erin would have loved this opportunity. He frowned, halting the memory as quickly as it sprung up. He had to retrain his mind to stop thinking about her. The separation was for her own good.

He arrived at the home for the sick children. The historic building was the stately home of a wealthy physician. The family trust had expanded on the property, making it into a small but renowned facility.

The ten acres of land on which the home sat was tended with the same level of care and attention that its residents received. Whenever he drove on the property, Marc felt as if he had escaped to a special, magical place that offered peace. There was something definitely serene and spiritual in the surroundings.

The staff was expecting him, and one of the nurses was on hand to greet him. She took him into the common room, where many of the more active children were involved with various tasks.

"Marc!" they called out to him once they noticed he was in the room.

"Yeah, I'm here. Good to see all of you." He hugged each of them as they waited for their turns. "I see a few new faces."

"Jamie is new," Todd responded. "And Patrick and Barbara."

"Welcome, newbies." He noted that they weren't as enthusiastic about his visit, although they were curious. "I'm going to make my rounds, visit with all of you and then come back here."

The nurse accompanied him on the rounds, per protocol. She introduced him to new patients, giving him a summary of their medical conditions. He held back any feelings of sorrow about their terminal status.

There was always room for hope. These children didn't deserve anyone giving up on them. He hadn't given up on his brother's ability to get better, even to the end.

Showing pity was doing a disservice to them. Despite their tiny frames, loss of hair, pale and sunken features, they were brave and had a hearty spirit for life. Visiting them and sharing kind words went a long way.

"Marc, you came back."

Seeing one of his favorite patients, an eleven-year-old boy, Marc hunkered down beside the child. "Hey, kiddo, I told you that I'd return." He offered the boy his baseball cap.

"I'm going home today."

"Really? Hot damn." He covered his mouth. "You didn't hear that."

"Bob is in remission." The nurse beside him beamed.

Marc hugged him. Suddenly he realized the impact of the news. Bob would return to his home in Montana.

Their budding friendship would have to withstand the physical separation.

"If I knew you were leaving, I'd have brought you a special treat."

"The only gift I want is for you to win the race tomorrow."

Marc looked into those eyes that regarded him with such high esteem. He couldn't let him down. He nodded.

Marc spent most of the morning visiting the rest of the hospital. He'd given some of the quieter ones his undivided attention. He wanted them to know that they could stand for what they believed in and that their dreams didn't need to be put on hold. Sometimes those dreams had the power to push back the disease.

Although his brother had succumbed to his illness, Marc considered it his duty to carry on their dream to be twin drivers and owners.

By the time he left the hospital, he had an armful of art, stuffed toys and handwritten poems to keep him company. The children were all so very dear to his heart. Even though he'd told himself to forget her, visiting them made him think of Erin even more.

Erin sat with her father in his apartment. Since she and Marc had decided to go their separate ways, Erin had a great desire to be with family. Last night Lani had joined her for pizza and a movie. Today she chose to hang out with her father and play one of his many board games.

She had no plans for tomorrow, the day that Marc would race.

Keeping her mind on the present, she stayed away from thinking about what he may be doing. How did drivers prepare? Did he have a ritual? Did he hang out with the guys? If she hadn't been so stubborn, she would know because she'd be in his life.

She had a nice long visit with her father, playing several games, sharing the home-cooked meal she made and trimming his hair while they caught up on national news.

"I have a confession." Her father made a face.

"What?"

"I'd heard that you have a boyfriend. I didn't want to pry. I tried to wait for you to share the news."

"That Lani has a big mouth."

"Please don't get angry. I like a bit of juicy gossip every now and again. Nothing much happening in these parts, except who's getting a hip replacement or a face-lift."

Erin laughed. "I hate to tell you, but my love life is even less interesting. And it's all past tense."

"Oh, dear, no."

Erin filled in her father with the details. She had nothing to hide. Lani had turned into her pushy self, urging her to make up with Marc after the race. According to Lani, she needed to get over it and deal with Marc's profession. However, Lani's motivation was a bit colored by the loss of access to the mansion.

Her father said nothing for a while. Erin thought that

maybe his mind had wandered. Maybe she should suggest another board game.

"I was thinking about your mom and me. Your story kind of reminded me of that."

"Really?" Erin still had her doubts that he was in the present.

"As you know, I retired from the Army Corps of Engineers."

Erin nodded.

"But I didn't join the military until after I'd married your mother. Gosh, she was angry."

"She didn't like the military."

"It wasn't that. She was pregnant with you and here I was signing up and heading out."

"I'm sure that didn't go down well."

"But I knew we needed money and stability, so I went for it. I didn't give her much choice. By the time I told her, I was shipping out the next week for boot camp."

Erin had never known that part of the story. But she couldn't see how this related to her situation.

"Your mom worried that something bad would happen to me. When it came time to re-up and I did, again she wondered why I would voluntarily sign up for that. Part of it was my duty. The other part is that I loved the military.

"She eventually came to terms. We had to do it together though. One person can't expect the other to go along without the other person's help."

Erin nodded. Philosophical discussions always

sounded good, far removed from the discussion in question. But it was a different thing sitting in front of Marc when tempers were raised.

Her father continued, "You can't wait for the right moment. You can't wait for a guaranteed outcome. If you want this young man, then walk that line of compromise and have some faith that he knows what he's doing."

"And who's going to have faith in me?"

"If what you said is true, he already has faith in you."

Marc took a seat behind the rows of microphones. Once more he questioned why he'd caved in to Martha's recommendation that he hold a press conference. The goal was for him to answer any questions about the gambling. More importantly, he needed to give his side of what he knew.

"Good morning, everyone." Marc had decided to write his statement so that he could make sure he covered all the necessary points. Plus he didn't want to wander off on a tangent if the media sharks smelled blood.

They listened attentively to his prepared statement. No one interrupted with questions. He managed to get out that he didn't know of or suspect Lionel's criminal activity. He would never condone such behavior. They had not spoken since his arrest, and he had complete confidence in his staff. Lionel was the anomaly to a perfect racing team.

Once he set down the paper, hands shot in the air.

Now came the hard part, where he may have to dance around negative or hostile questions. Martha had provided a list of reporters who had supported him throughout the ordeal.

He selected those hands for the first round. Taking several deep breaths, he settled in for the barrage of questions. Some reporters grilled him about the gambling ring; others questioned whether he had the right team to get him into the top three position.

It didn't take long before he'd had enough. His head pounded, and he struggled to keep any sign of impatience from his demeanor.

Thankfully, Martha stepped up and skillfully ended the press conference. She patted him on the shoulder. "You did fine," she whispered. "Let's get out of here."

"I'm feeling old all of a sudden. This is worse than going around the track. I could be running the business in peace and let a younger, hungrier driver take over the spotlight."

"Shhh. Someone may hear you." Martha gripped his elbow and ushered him away from the mics.

Marc had erupted with his private misgivings. He didn't mean for anyone, even Martha, to hear. But as empty as he felt, he couldn't pretend that all of this had any meaning without Erin.

Priorities had shifted. He now realized that the natural process had scared the mess out of him. His foot-stomping and belligerent attitude had occurred because of the scary feeling that change was in the air.

Pushing aside Erin to get back that stability had been

the biggest mistake. Once this race was over, he'd do whatever it took to get her back.

Loving her didn't mean that it was all or nothing. His little friends in the hospital unknowingly had taught him that blessings shouldn't be ignored or taken for granted. Erin Wilson was his biggest blessing.

Erin texted Wallace when she arrived at the arena. She counted herself lucky for having such a supporter in her corner. Otherwise the already difficult task to convince Marc that she belonged in his life would be more difficult.

"Did he respond?" Lani asked at her side.

"Not yet."

They waited at the entrance gate. While she waited for Wallace to arrive with their tickets, she noted the exuberant crowds flowing into the arena. The crowd spanned all demographics. Women, men, kids with their parents and grandparents to singles to senior citizens. The sport attracted a diverse crowd, all a little rabid in her opinion.

Her phone buzzed, announcing Wallace was looking for them. They coordinated the details and finally connected.

"My favorite young ladies are here. Let's get to the box."

Lani and Wallace walked ahead a bit. Her sister fired so many questions at Wallace that Erin felt sorry for the man.

Erin noted the heightened excitement that electrified

the air. She figured a person had to be coldhearted or dead to not surrender to the celebratory atmosphere. People grouped in twos, threes or in large social circles. Their lively conversation centered around the industry news, statistics on their favorite drivers or plain trash talk.

The redolent smell of stadium food permeated the air. She passed a hot dog vendor and suddenly craved a hot, juicy one loaded with everything messy and gooey. However, she passed on the purchase rather than spend the afternoon with indigestion.

She craned her neck, looking for the areas where the pit crews worked.

"Marc's team is at the end there." Wallace pointed off to the left. He loaned her his binoculars. For several minutes, she surveyed the area where all the teams busily prepared their cars. She only looked for one person. Then she saw him. Her heart hitched with recognition as she zoomed in on her target.

Despite the fear of him rejecting her once more, seeing him solidified her proposed action. She wanted her man, every part of him.

Chapter 11

Marc stayed far away from anyone leading up to this moment. Race day had arrived with unseasonable warmth for mid-November. Clouds had settled in, promising rain. So far, no precipitation had fallen and that spelled good news for the track.

Today was not any race day. The last day of the professional car racing season had particular significance. Final rankings for the season would be determined. Start positions for the next season earned. This was a championship race.

The new car under his power had been fitted, refitted and designed to all his needs. Nothing was too much for him to get a win. And he wanted the title like a hungry tiger homing in on its dinner.

Many other drivers would have the same mind-set.

They had no choice but to come to the speedway with their A game. Like any other sport with athletes psyching themselves up, raging to get the full adrenaline load, pushing through to reach that mental zone, the professional drivers created and followed their prerace routines. Vigor, stamina and willingness to fight for every mile made the difference between who snagged the top spots and who went home defeated.

Cars jockeying for position would be aggressive and ruthless. Red flags would be seen throughout the race. This wasn't a day where pure aggression would be the winning strategy. Mental toughness and acuity mattered in order to outwit those drivers hungry for a win.

Pressure built within him—from the race and from the turmoil in his private world. The extent of Lionel's scandal had left his staff shaken. His previous disastrous runs hung over his head, a constant reminder of failure. Inner demons of doubt that were always resurrected prior to a race tried to shake his resolve.

He waited in the pit for his turn. His team had practiced their timing and maneuvers to get his car in and out of the pit. A few nights they had surprised him with a visit to the house to have a pep rally of sorts. Thank goodness he didn't have any close neighbors for all the hoopla that had occurred.

So many times he shared his admiration for their work ethic and their loyalty. Quite unexpectedly they had shared how much his leadership meant to them. No matter what Lionel's impact would be, they were a family who would stick together. Their unity and belief in his leadership had choked him up yesterday. Today, the sentiment added a boost to bolster his determination.

A young high school girl stepped up to the podium and belted out "The Star Spangled Banner." Even before she finished, the crowd erupted in applause that she'd managed to sing it beautifully and without forgetting the words.

Marc took a deep breath and put on his helmet. Immediately the sound was muted. His gloved hands flexed to ease the tension. He rolled his neck and kicked out each leg. A twinge, small enough to catch his attention, pulled at his neck.

Training had been intense. He was ready. Every muscle, every bone, ligament, tendon had been worked and prepped for the extreme forces that would be launched against his body. Lean and mean came to mind for how his body looked.

One of the celebrated professional wrestlers took the place of the singer. He served as grand marshall over the event. In a loud, booming voice, he announced, "Start your engines."

Marc locked in his focus straight ahead. He moved his car into the start position following the black-and-white pace car. They made the perfunctory lap before the pace car pulled off onto the pit road. The green flag was raised and swooped down.

For Marc, the crowd disappeared. All he saw was the length of the speedway, blacktopped and treacherous. He noted the other drivers in his periphery. He'd be damned if he got blindsided again. But he wasn't going to give any of them the power by strategizing a race against them. This was a showdown with him and the speedway.

Cars slingshot out, their drivers pushing down on the gas. Marc hit the road and didn't look back. His car rumbled with a vibration akin to a rocket engine. He bore down on his opponents, shifting and blocking, slowing down to then shift gears and shoot out in front.

Two hundred laps. Three hundred miles. He would eat up the distance one mile at a time averaging one hundred and seventy miles per hour. Caution flags flashed and he obeyed, getting off the track when cars left debris. It wasn't uncommon for cars to skim the retaining wall as they went too high on the track to make a power move.

Another hazard was the blinding sunset that lingered over the first turn. The crew had taped an automotive-grade adhesive to the windshield to eliminate the glare, and his helmet also had a peel-away film to soften the brightness. Luckily the obstruction would only last the first half hour of the race. However, thirty minutes was long enough to miscalculate to his detriment. Marc shifted his car behind the few cars in the lead, allowing them to be his shield.

The new car handled like a breeze for the most part. He only made one unscheduled stop at the pit, to change the fuel pump gauge. He'd taken a penalty for that, but it couldn't be helped.

The pit road speed limit dropped to forty-five miles per hour. Many drivers earned penalties for driving too fast coming into their pit area or taking off to rejoin the team of cars. Marc made sure to stay in the speed limit not one minute too late or too soon.

His pit crew's performance was stellar. He wasn't disappointed when he had to pull in twice for tire changes and to pull out a bumper after he'd hit a car to make a point. His pit chief deserved a fat bonus for having the guys operate with military precision around the car, each person on one task. Their choreographed moves cut down on wasted seconds, allowing him to stay in the game.

Occasionally he got thirsty and sipped from his specially designed cup. But he didn't think about eating at a time like this. His energy never flagged. His focus never wavered. The hours slipped by with ease. He was used to the grind, lap after lap, and he wanted to be nowhere else but on the speedway.

Finally, he approached the final turn. His car was in a heated dogfight, nose to nose.

His spotter spoke to him through his mic, alerting him of any hidden dangers. Lionel was supposed to be the spotter for this race. Another driver who wasn't racing had stepped up to take his place. The kind gesture made a deep impact on Marc. The inner circle was opening its ranks to let him stand beside them. Maybe he had finally paid his dues.

Marc closed the gap next to his car. He turned on the aggression in an effort to test and even to scare the driver. Once upon a time, he was the rookie. His nerves had been repeatedly tested until he pushed back to show that he had the *cojones* to scrap with the best of them.

This driver was new on the scene. Marc didn't plan to show any mercy. Time for him to know what driving with the big dogs was all about. They could drink beer afterward and talk about the race. Right now, he was taking everybody out that stood in his way.

Marc sensed that the driver would pull back seconds before he actually did. Those precious seconds provided him with just enough advancement to push his car forward, squeezing the less experienced driver back, and overtake him through a narrow gauntlet of cars.

One down. Marc had two more obstacles to get around. So close, he could almost taste it. His breathing adjusted. Small threads of panic started in his gut. Now was not the time to choke. Critics had given him that reputation, a bit unfairly, he liked to think. Failure would be a bitter pill. He had no appetite for second or even third best.

"Focus!" he screamed the order.

"Yeah, get your head out your wazoo," his spotter yelled, adding a few more expletives.

"Matt, this is for you!" He thought about his brother, their dream. "I need you now, bro."

The steering wheel continued to vibrate in his hands. This car was alive and responding to his slightest touch. All the tools to win were in his control. His mind cleared away the fear like sunshine pushing through dank fog. His breathing grew calm. A meditative chant made a rhythmic beat in his head.

He steered the car from one side to the other in a daring diagonal move.

One car in his wake smelled his exhaust fumes.

One more to go.

The driver ahead was a veteran. In the business, Marc was the young pup against this man's legacy. But there could only be one at the top of the mountain. This was a hostile takeover.

In a David versus Goliath moment, Marc opened the throttle. He urged the car not to spin out, but to push forward like a winner. He gripped the wheel with enough power to steer but loose enough to let the car run free.

The race would be close. But close didn't count, at least not today. He continued pushing, even when the checkered flag waved at him as he crossed the finish line first.

The victory lap was like nectar from the gods. Marc drove the special lap in a state of disbelief, mixed with straight-up glee, and with a whole lot of gratitude to his brother, who he knew had helped him on that track.

The crowd had not stopped cheering. He waved to them, truly appreciative of their support. Signs of "Maverick" waved at him. Once a label he'd grown uncomfortable with, the name now suited him and his team. They had firmly established that they were here to stay.

Finally he exited the car. His crew surrounded him, ready to hoist him onto their shoulders. He had a feeling that he'd be celebrating for several days.

"Hey, guys, put me down." Marc hoped that he wasn't having some postrace hallucination. He couldn't believe that he was watching Erin running at full speed toward him.

He broke away from his men, running toward her.

Erin had come. She'd seen the race.

They collided with exclamations of joy. She jumped into his arms in a full-on tackle, almost knocking them over.

"Oh, my gosh, that was awesome," she exclaimed. Her heartbeat thudded against his chest.

"It did feel good. You feel good." He set her down but didn't let go. He never wanted to let go again.

"Mr. Newton," a reporter called out. "Heard that you're going to retire. Say it ain't so."

Erin stepped back to study Marc's face. "Marc? You can't walk away from this. Please tell me that he's wrong. I won't let you give up your dream."

He returned her gaze, which reflected her pride. His heart swelled that his woman was at his side for one of the most important days in his career.

She didn't realize that she cried until he wiped a tear from her cheek. "It's okay."

She shook her head. "No." She cleared her throat and looked directly at the reporter. "No, he's not retiring. He's still creating his legacy in a sport he loves. You'll be seeing more of Marc Newton."

"And who are you, miss?"

Before Erin could answer, Marc spoke up. "She's soon to be my wife…if she'll have me."

"Miss?" The reporter clearly loved being at the center of a news-making moment.

"Yes. I'd be proud to be his wife."

"You may kiss the bride-to-be," the reporter prompted. His cameraman documented the moment.

Marc scooped her up in a bear hug. Her feet dangled as she held on tightly around his neck. From her lofty position, she met his mouth and joined him in a full, deep kiss.

They broke apart when the first dousing of champagne occurred. Standing next to him completely, she shared in the congratulations for the double celebration. He couldn't have planned it any other way.

When they had a moment to themselves, Erin leaned close to his ear. "Were you really going to retire?"

"I'd have done anything to keep you happy."

"Not at the expense of such a sacrifice. I love everything about you, just the way you are. I love all that you do, in and out of the spotlight. What I feel about your profession is natural, but today when I saw you on the track, I saw a phenomenon. You live and breathe this world. And it has added to your character. That's what I'd fallen in love with back then. Nothing has changed."

"Baby, I lost my mind from the first time that I saw you. I couldn't imagine a moment without you in my life. My heart, body and soul are yours. Only you are the center of my world. I love you so much." He knelt in front of her. His face turned up toward hers, the depth of his love plain on his face. "I can't wait to make this official. I want you in my life, so we can laugh and love for years and years to come. But more urgently than that, I look forward to holding you in my arms in front of the fire at home, void of clothing, in the next couple of hours."

Erin gave him the biggest smile. "Race you there."

* * * * *

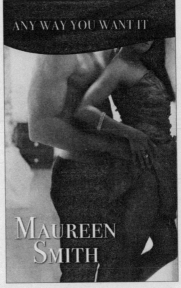

REQUEST YOUR FREE BOOKS!

2 FREE NOVELS
PLUS 2 FREE GIFTS!

KIMANI
ROMANCE ™

Love's ultimate destination!

YES! Please send me 2 FREE Kimani™ Romance novels and my 2 FREE gifts (gifts are worth about $10). After receiving them, if I don't wish to receive any more books, I can return the shipping statement marked "cancel." If I don't cancel, I will receive 4 brand-new novels every month and be billed just $4.94 per book in the U.S. or $5.49 per book in Canada. That's a saving of at least 21% off the cover price. It's quite a bargain! Shipping and handling is just 50¢ per book in the U.S. and 75¢ per book in Canada.* I understand that accepting the 2 free books and gifts places me under no obligation to buy anything. I can always return a shipment and cancel at any time. Even if I never buy another book, the two free books and gifts are mine to keep forever.

168/368 XDN FEJR

Name	(PLEASE PRINT)	

Address		Apt. #

City	State/Prov.	Zip/Postal Code

Signature (if under 18, a parent or guardian must sign)

Mail to the **Reader Service:**
IN U.S.A.: P.O. Box 1867, Buffalo, NY 14240-1867
IN CANADA: P.O. Box 609, Fort Erie, Ontario L2A 5X3

Not valid for current subscribers to Kimani Romance books.

Want to try two free books from another line?
Call 1-800-873-8635 or visit www.ReaderService.com.

* Terms and prices subject to change without notice. Prices do not include applicable taxes. Sales tax applicable in N.Y. Canadian residents will be charged applicable taxes. Offer not valid in Quebec. This offer is limited to one order per household. All orders subject to credit approval. Credit or debit balances in a customer's account(s) may be offset by any other outstanding balance owed by or to the customer. Please allow 4 to 6 weeks for delivery. Offer available while quantities last.

Your Privacy—The Reader Service is committed to protecting your privacy. Our Privacy Policy is available online at www.ReaderService.com or upon request from the Reader Service.

We make a portion of our mailing list available to reputable third parties that offer products we believe may interest you. If you prefer that we not exchange your name with third parties, or if you wish to clarify or modify your communication preferences, please visit us at www.ReaderService.com/consumerschoice or write to us at Reader Service Preference Service, P.O. Box 9062, Buffalo, NY 14269. Include your complete name and address.

KROM11B